DOUBLE DUTCH

⊰ STORIES ⊱

DOUBLE DUTCH

⚔ STORIES ⚕

LAURA TRUNKEY

Published in Canada in 2016 by House of Anansi Press Inc.
www.houseofanansi.com

House of Anansi Press is committed to protecting our natural
environment. As part of our efforts, the interior of this book is printed on
paper that contains 100% post-consumer recycled fibres, is acid-free, and is
processed chlorine-free.

20 19 18 17 16   1 2 3 4 5

Library and Archives Canada Cataloguing in Publication

Trunkey, Laura, author
Double Dutch / Laura Trunkey.

Short stories.
Issued in print and electronic formats.
ISBN 978-1-77089-877-6 (paperback).—ISBN 978-1-77089-878-3 (html)

I. Title.

PS8639.R85D69 2016   C813'.6   C2015-907617-X
                                             C2015-907618-8

"Hands Like Birds" previously appeared in *Grain* issue 32.7
"Ursus Arctos Horribilis" previously appeared in *Border Crossings* issue 116
"Double Dutch" previously appeared in *Prairie Fire* issue 33.2
"Second Comings and Goings" previously appeared in *Grain* issue 39.1
"Winchester .30-.30" previously appeared in *The Malahat Review* issue 179

Cover and text design: Alysia Shewchuk

*We acknowledge for their financial support of our publishing program the Canada
Council for the Arts, the Ontario Arts Council, and the Government of Canada
through the Canada Book Fund.*

Printed and bound in Canada

MIX
Paper from
responsible sources
FSC® C004071
www.fsc.org

⚖ CONTENTS

CONTENTS

for MAM

⚔ **NIGHT TERROR**

He was speaking Arabic in his sleep. Her son—who could barely manage three words in a row in English—had an incredible fluency in a language she recognized only from television news clips.

"Are there Arabic children here?" Nicole asked one of the daycare workers when she dropped Jasper off the next morning. The worker had an undercut and one of those disorienting genderless names: Leslie or Jamie or Alex. She—Nicole guessed—had a stud in her nose, which was small and not entirely tasteless. But Leslie/Jamie/Alex looked at Nicole and raised her eyebrows in a way Nicole expected she probably raised her eyebrows at her toddler charges—when they got faux nut butter embedded in their hair, when they had particularly malodorous bowel movements. And then she walked away. She thought Nicole was a racist, obviously. And Nicole was not a racist. The only reason she couldn't claim any ethnic friends was that she had no friends to claim, period.

But in her frequent encounters with restaurant delivery drivers she was social and tipped well. Also, her assistant, Anita, whose work ethic was lacking but whose banter she enjoyed, was half Chinese.

"There are a couple of Pakis," whispered a father beside her, a man in a business suit with a soft face that did not suit his word choice. "But from what I can tell, they're pretty civilized." *This man*, she wanted to scream, *is the racist*. But instead she thanked him and then stepped far way. She looked for Jasper in the large playroom. He was building block piles and smashing them down. Normal two-year-old behaviour, according to the staff. She went to work.

Jasper was a problem child. The daycare workers used the words *energetic* and *expressive*, but Nicole knew what they were implying. She suspected the staff held daily meetings to select the issue to be brought to her attention and the euphemistic language to employ when describing it: *Jasper was distracted during quiet time*. Translation: Jasper kept the rest of the toddlers awake. *We are working with Jasper on asking before taking*. Translation: Jasper spent his day ripping toys from other little hands. And a frequent one: *Jasper was physical*. This, Nicole knew, was code for *violent*.

These understatements were likely an attempt at kindness, but kindness wasn't helpful. It was best when people were direct. After all, it wasn't as though Jasper's behaviour was a surprise to Nicole. She lived with him. Yesterday, another *physical* day, when Nicole overheard a girl tell her mom she'd been shoved off the slide, she'd watched her son glance quickly in her direction and then away. She could read that look. He had been the perpetrator.

When Jasper was younger, before she'd thought better of it, Nicole had taken him to kindergym. She had seen children push dolls around the gymnasium in buggies rather than hurl them off playground equipment. She had seen them throw balls to—rather than at—each other. She had seen them successfully keep their hands to themselves. Also, she had seen them hug their mothers without being coerced. No matter how typical the daycare workers claimed Jasper's behaviour was, Nicole knew the truth.

One problem with being a single parent was not having anyone to talk to about things that mattered, or at least anyone who shared her values, anyone who made sense to her. After a week of Arabic, she called her mother.

"How can you tell it's Arabic?" Sylvia asked.

"That's what it sounds like."

"How are you the expert? Do you speak Arabic, Nicole? Do you even know any Arabs?"

"Jesus, Mom." She was about to hang up when Sylvia had another coughing fit. She never bothered to cover the receiver. Nicole could picture her, her arm stretched to hold the phone away but her head still turned to face it. The fit lasted three minutes. Nicole timed it on the second hand of her watch, the whole time shouting advice: *Have a glass of water, Mom. Or a lozenge. Aren't there Fisherman's Friends in the cabinet in the bathroom? Or honey. Do you have any honey?* When she did finally hang up, it was with twice as many things to worry about.

She wished she had sisters. The whole point of siblings was commiseration, people who had been screwed up in precisely the same ways and therefore understood you on a level no one else could. Or at least that's how she imagined it. But Nicole was alone in the world. And she couldn't tell her mother her suspicion: her son was the reincarnation of an Arab. And—judging by Jasper's tendency for violence, his lack of empathy—this Arab had been a terrorist.

Sylvia's neighbour, Mrs. Rose, had taken a tarot workshop last year and ever since had been asking to read Nicole's cards. Two weeks after the nighttime Arabic began, Nicole agreed. She figured it was possible that a woman with such a keen interest in predicting the future might be equally interested in predicting the past.

Nicole sat across from Mrs. Rose with a cup of camomile tea, a half-dozen cards spread before her on the table. Jasper was there too, but she had brought the playpen. When he went to other people's houses, he had a habit of breaking their prized possessions. "Do you know anything about reincarnation?"

Mrs. Rose's eyes were fireworks. "In my past life, I was a French cellist. And I was abused by my husband, which is why I have such trust issues when it comes to men. Always have."

"How do you know this?" Nicole asked.

"Hypnosis. Past-life regression. I saw an expert."

"Do they do children?" Nicole asked.

Mrs. Rose turned to Jasper. He had his hand over the side of the playpen, on an afghan. Nicole grabbed the blanket away before Mrs. Rose could notice that he'd begun to unravel the corner. "I don't know," she said. "Maybe."

The expert didn't do children. "Two?" she repeated when Nicole called her.

"Two and a half," Nicole said.

"Um, nope." She said it like she thought Nicole was crazy. Nicole crazy? This woman hypnotized people to reveal they were French cellists with trust issues. Though Nicole supposed she was a little bit crazy. She had spent the last week on the computer searching for a terrorist with a date of death that corresponded with Jasper's birth-date. Osama bin Laden had died fourteen months before Jasper was born, not that she suspected Jasper was the reincarnation of Osama bin Laden. Though there was that thing he did with his Lego airplane.

Maybe she didn't need a corresponding death date. She called the woman again.

"Say someone dies. Do they get reincarnated that day, or is there a waiting period?"

"Obviously, there is some specific famous person you hope your kid is."

"Oh no," Nicole said. "I don't hope. It's the opposite of hope."

"Look, I don't just dole out information over the phone. If you have questions, book an appointment. For yourself."

The woman clearly hated her. Nicole made an appointment for Monday morning.

Nicole hadn't loved Jasper right away. In the beginning, she was unable to love anything. She felt, most of the time, the precise opposite of the mothers in the diaper ads. The ones with waistlines and perky, unengorged breasts, their smooth faces displaying equal parts serenity and adoration. But it wasn't specifically about Jasper. It was because depression ran in her family, the doctor said. And because she'd had that problem herself in high school. And because she was parenting on her own, Jasper's father being an old boyfriend from college who was separated but with a tan line on his ring finger, and who hadn't been worth more than one drunken, fumbling mistake. And because she didn't tell him. Didn't tell anyone, so that her mother assumed Nicole was promiscuous. And lectured Nicole about the risks of promiscuity — aside from the obvious, experienced risk — when in truth she had slept with only three men in her life.

There were pills for the depression. Of course, there

are also pills for pregnancy, if one suspects it soon enough. And if one reacts in the way unattached, unprepared women are expected to react. Which is badly, and not the way she had reacted, which was to order a subscription to *Fit Pregnancy* and rearrange her work schedule to accommodate daily prenatal yoga classes. To reimagine her life with a purpose.

Nicole didn't want to take pills for the depression. She had held off for what felt like forever. Months, weeks, maybe it was only days. There was a counsellor in a small, windowless room who put her hand on Nicole's arm when she cried, her body racked with sobs as Jasper squirmed in his bassinet on the floor beside her. The woman's nails were painted a different colour every session. Flawless nails that Nicole suspected for weeks were artificial, until the day she noticed a spot of polish on the counsellor's cuticle. There was a support group also. But the women were always talking about how their husbands just didn't get it—their husbands, their husbands, their husbands— until Nicole couldn't sit through a meeting without muttering strings of obscenities under her breath.

It was possible that she had been depressed because subconsciously she knew the truth. She recognized Jasper for what he really was.

But Nicole loved Jasper now. She did. She had always wondered: men in jail—not the white-collar criminals, but the murderers, the rapists—who would visit them? Besides the sicko women who were into that kind of thing. But now she understood: not just sicko women, but mothers also. Unless that was one and the same.

Not to say that it was easy to accept being the mother of a problem child. To have other mothers judge her the way they were always judging her. As if it were Jasper's home life that was the problem, or, more specifically, as if his problem was *her*. But that was Motherhood: a life-long marathon of sizing up the competition. Nicole hated mothers. In general, fathers too. She stopped taking Jasper to kindergym primarily because of the other mothers and the way they'd look at Nicole when Jasper clamped his mouth on the arms of their precious darlings. And this when he didn't even have teeth!

In recalling kindergym, it dawned on Nicole that she had overlooked key facts. The first child Jasper bit was Eli something-or-other, his distraught mother graced with a very prominent nose. The second child, the grandson of her mother's optometrist, had the last name of Weinstein.

She had Anita clear her schedule for Monday morning. This, she said, because she had an appointment with a specialist regarding her son.

"Is it serious?" Anita asked. She had been playing Spider Solitaire on the computer, and didn't even bother to sink the screen.

Nicole only nodded, and then ducked into her office, leaving Anita to stare after her, her expression a mix of sympathy and speculation.

Nicole considered asking Anita to clear her entire week.

It was always the same: briefs to write, briefings on said briefs, revisions to said briefs, over and over and over. Before motherhood, she'd been impressed with herself. Her salary, her office, the fact that she had someone to answer her phone — this all meant she was successful. But that wasn't true. When she was at work she was bored, and when she was home she was unstable. She couldn't make a decision without second-guessing herself. And every decision she did make had negative repercussions. That she had given Jasper yogurt and fruit when he wouldn't eat even a bite of his dinner meant he now never ate anything for dinner but yogurt and fruit. That she let him watch Thomas the Train episodes on her laptop meant that every time she needed to finish something at home, he would shriek for the computer and smash the keys. That she bribed him with fish crackers meant that he wouldn't do anything she asked without the promise of "cracko snacks."

Before the Arabic, Nicole often sat in the glide rocker in Jasper's room once he fell asleep. He had never been a particularly sweet child. Even in infancy, he would not cuddle. When she tried, he'd arch away from her, his body rigid. He'd flail his arms and legs when she changed his diaper, and laugh when he made contact with her stomach. And then there was the breastfeeding. First it was the fingernails to her chest, such fierce scratches from such delicate weapons. Once his first two teeth grew in, at ten months, she had transitioned to the bottle.

He was rarely violent with Nicole anymore, but he wasn't affectionate. She watched the other parents at daycare scoop their children into their arms and kiss them. When she tried this with Jasper, he'd wriggle free. When she read to him, he sat beside her on the couch, never on her lap. He held her hand when she made him, but generally she ended up with his wrist only, or his sleeve. But when he was asleep, she could pretend. She'd stand over him, his hair plastered to his forehead, his pyjamas twisted around his legs, his mouth-wide-open rasps. *My precious boy*, she'd whisper, and he wouldn't even squirm.

But once the Arabic began, she could not stand to be near him at night. Certainly he still looked the same, but what she saw was different: his skin turned darker and turtle-rough, his eyebrows thick, a sneer on his lips.

Before Jasper, Nicole had believed in nurture over nature, but Jasper unravelled this hypothesis. She had made mistakes with Jasper, maybe more mistakes than average, but she could not have brought this on herself. She had worked so hard to do things right. Even when she was miserable, she had held herself somewhat together for his sake. She had followed the rules for umbilical hygiene, for vaccinations, for tummy time, for the painfully slow introduction of solids. She had taken him to crawl around with other babies when she didn't want to leave the house. She had gotten up every thirty minutes for months instead of letting him cry it out, because her yoga teacher had given her an article that compared sleep training to the abandonment of children in Russian orphanages. She had sacrificed sanity to supply her son with every building block required for a perfect beginning, to guarantee he would turn out right. And it hadn't worked.

Wanda the hypnotist was her mother's age, and had a lady's mullet. Her pants and shirt were different shades of denim. Nicole had been hoping for something different, something she could take seriously.

"I request payment upfront," Wanda said, ushering Nicole towards a La-Z-Boy in the centre of the living room. The worn brown upholstery was covered in cat fur.

Nicole pulled six twenties from her wallet. This was not a purchase she wished to leave evidence of in the form of a cheque. Wanda counted the bills, then rolled them into a tight tube and tucked them in her shirt pocket.

Nicole glanced at the chair. The cat hair was thick. Also white, while Nicole's pants were black. "Before we start, can I just ask you some questions?"

"That'll be included in your hour."

"And also, do you have a blanket or something? Only that I have to go to work after…" She waved her hand at the chair.

Wanda breathed sharply out her nose, then disappeared down a hallway.

Yes, definitely she hated her. But how could this

woman expect a visitor—a customer—to sit on a mat of cat fur? Still, maybe she should have said she was allergic.

Wanda came back and handed Nicole a Coors Light beach towel. She sat down across from her on a swivel office chair.

"You told my neighbour she had been a cellist, with trust issues," Nicole said, then waited for something in return. A nod, or some sign that Wanda—who was stroking the overweight Siamese in her lap—was engaged in the conversation. She got nothing.

"And obviously the cellist thing didn't transfer to this lifetime. I mean, she doesn't play the cello. But she still has the trust issues. Apparently."

Wanda continued to pat the cat, who was now draped belly-up across her lap. They were the worst cats, Siamese. So bad-tempered.

"So?" Nicole asked.

"Was that a question?" Wanda asked.

At a rate of two dollars a minute, Nicole had probably paid for three meals for the purring monster. And gotten nothing in return. "What I'm saying," she tried again, "is that some things transferred but some things didn't. And I'm wondering if that's always how it is."

"Did you play an instrument as a child?" Wanda was looking at Nicole now, the first time she'd made eye contact. She had violet eyes. On anyone else Nicole would have assumed they were contacts, but on a woman dressed in double denim that hypothesis seemed less likely.

"I played the flute in grade six. In band."

"And can you still play?" She was honed in on Nicole now. Was that how she did the hypnosis—those unblinking purple eyes?

Nicole lowered her gaze to the cat. "I doubt it."

"Did you ever have a traumatic experience as a child?" The cat slipped off Wanda's lap and slunk to the corner of the room. It licked its paw.

Nicole thought of her mother picking her up from school in grade three, barely room in the car with the garbage bags stuffed full of their possessions. Nicole saying, *but Daddy, but Daddy,* and her mother responding, *Fuck your father!*

She pushed down the cuticles on her right hand with her left thumbnail. "I guess," she said finally.

"And does it still affect you?"

Her mother's theory was that it was Nicole's father's fault that Nicole was bad at relationships—poor role-modelling. Though wouldn't her mother be equally culpable? From her, Nicole had picked up her nonchalance. Her belief in the pointlessness of putting in effort. Nicole shrugged.

"Even in the course of a lifetime, we forget things. The flute playing, for example. Whereas some experiences imprint themselves on the deepest level of our beings. These are the type of things that follow us from one life to the next."

"Huh." On some horrifying level, this made sense. Nicole was doomed to lifetimes of failed relationships, and Jasper was doomed to lifetimes of terrorism. "My son speaks Arabic," she said. "In his sleep."

Wanda was silent, then she stood and disappeared down the hall again. Was this Nicole's cue to leave? That the past-life hypnotist had declared Nicole to be the lunatic? But then she came back with a dog-eared paperback. "It's a heavily documented phenomenon," she said, handing Nicole the book.

"*The Journey of Your Soul*," Nicole read aloud. One seemingly safe bet she would have made even a couple of months back was that she would never lay hands on a book with *Soul* in the title, especially one classified as non-fiction.

"I've never encountered it myself, but it's fascinating."

"That's one word for it," Nicole said. It was a relief to be believed, but she wondered if it should have been. Considering the audience. "It's not the Arabic that bothers me, but what goes along with it. I mean, I love my son, but he's not a nice boy."

"Toddlers aren't nice," Wanda said. "Believe me. I endured three of my own, and now I'm reliving it through my grandsons."

"He hits other children."

"Exactly."

"And bites."

"Been there. Hard enough to draw blood," Wanda said. "And my daughter was a spitter."

Every parent had their own behaviour horror stories, even the ones who pretended they didn't. But how to explain that this was not simply bad behaviour? "He stacks things: blocks, books, couch cushions. And then he plows them down." She paused. "With a Lego airplane. While making exploding sounds."

Wanda snorted. Nicole glanced up at her. Her fist was pressed against her mouth. She was suppressing a laugh.

"It's not amusing."

Wanda nodded, looked away. Inhaled a deep breath. "Of course not. Only I'm sure your son isn't the reincarnation of Osama bin Laden."

"I'm not saying he is. Though if reincarnation is a fact, then someone's kid has to be."

"Well, not necessarily. There are different theories."

Nicole stood, folded the towel, and placed the book on top. "I should go back to work."

"You still have forty minutes. We could do a short session. Delve into your pasts to discover the root of this anxiety."

Nicole shook her head, then darted to the door.

"How's Jasper?" Anita asked when she arrived at work.

Nicole shrugged. "Same as usual." The last time she'd taken Jasper to the office, Anita had insisted on holding him on her lap. He had not protested as Anita hoisted him by his armpits, and for a brief, blissful moment Nicole had thought she'd found an adult Jasper responded well to. A human being Jasper liked. But then he'd hooked his finger into Anita's hoop earring and ripped it from her earlobe. There had been blood.

"But the specialist..."

"The specialist was no help at all," Nicole said. "She was a charlatan."

"I don't want to pry..." Anita began. Which was obviously untrue. Anita loved to pry. She knew the business of everyone in the office, a fact that Nicole often benefited from. "But is he sick?"

"I don't know," Nicole said. "I mean, not physically."

"Do you maybe want to talk about it?"

Nicole shook her head and ducked into her office. She stared at the picture of Jasper on her desk. He was wearing a fluorescent orange bike helmet and smiling. Jasper seldom smiled, though Sylvia claimed this was not the case around her. *You can't be afraid to be silly with him, sweetheart. Just muck about and make a mess.* Nicole had tried this: vrooming as she skidded Hot Wheels across the living room, pudding painting on the deck while Jasper eyed her skeptically. Even with only her son for an audience, she felt self-conscious. The same way she did when she followed the public health nurse's advice and maintained a running monologue, referring to herself in the third person. *Now Mommy is going into the kitchen. She is taking Jasper's sippy cup from the dishwater. She is turning on the tap and waiting for the water to get cold.* Normal dialogue with Jasper was almost as awkward. He rarely looked up, and his infrequent replies never surpassed two syllables. Nicole kept the radios in the house and the car tuned to talk stations, to model conversation. Also for a semblance of companionship.

There was a peal of laughter outside her office door: Anita. Nicole glanced at the photo again, then flipped it over. Probably Sylvia pressed the shutter just after Jasper threw a stone from the rock garden at her Shih Tzu.

She didn't want to talk to Anita, because Anita was her assistant. Because there was such a thing as professional distance. Because Anita had a big mouth. But it was also a fact that Anita was the closest thing she had to a friend, if a friend was someone whose company you enjoyed on a regular basis. The friends she hadn't alienated in her year of postnatal misery she had alienated afterwards, when she chose to decline all social events rather than be judged on her son's behaviour. The only person outside of work she frequently spent time with was Sylvia. And though her mother would love it, it was a bit too pathetic to refer to her as a friend.

Nicole pressed the button on the phone. "Anita, could you come here?"

Anita knocked once on the door, then let herself in. "Yes?"

"Do you want to sit down?"

Anita sat. She was chewing gum. Was that unprofessional? Would people on the phone be able to tell that Anita had something in her mouth? Or if she squirrelled it in her cheek, would no one know the difference? The latter, Nicole decided. Though if someone ever complained, of course she'd have to speak to her about it.

Anita, seeming to read her mind, or noticing her star-ing at her mouth, took a tissue from her pocket and spat her gum into it. "It's Nicorette," she said.

"Oh," Nicole said. "That's great, Anita. Good for you." Patronizing. Definitely that was patronizing, but Anita didn't seem to notice.

"Wait until I've lasted forty-eight hours before you congratulate me."

Nicole nodded. She rummaged in her desk drawer for nothing in particular.

"Did you want me to help you with something?" Anita asked.

"Oh, no," Nicole said. "I mean, yes. Well, I just thought. Do you know anything about Arabic?"

Anita laughed. "I know absolutely nothing about Arabic. Do you need something translated? I could find you someone."

"Translated? Huh. Maybe."

"Just let me know." Anita picked up the picture of Jasper that was face down on the desk. She tilted it towards her and smiled, then spun it so it faced Nicole again. "Are you okay, Nicole? Are you sure there isn't anything you want to talk about?"

"Jasper's a terror—" Nicole clamped her mouth shut before the third syllable escaped.

But Anita just nodded. "The terrible twos."

Nicole shrugged. She was trying to decide whether a translator would be useful. She could tape Jasper, but that would mean setting up camp in his bedroom. Also, it was distinctly likely that knowing what he was saying would be worse than not knowing.

"It must be super hard, doing it all by yourself," Anita said.

It was super hard. It was. But unfortunately, Nicole's body agreed with this statement by way of tears. An unstaunchable tear cascade. She tried to press them away with the back of her hand, but this did nothing. She gulped a sob, then spun her chair to face the wall. She wiped her cheeks with her sleeve and took a couple of slow, deep breaths.

Anita stood and put her arms around Nicole's shoulders. "I'm so in awe of you. Single mom. Professional woman. And to top it all off, always so put together."

"Put together?" Nicole sniffed. "That's laughable."

"Not at all," Anita said. "What you need is a break. A week on a beach somewhere. Or barring that, at least a night out."

"Probably," Nicole said.

"So I'll babysit," Anita said. "Friday night, 7 p.m. until whenever you get home. And I won't take no for an answer."

"I'm serious, Anita. He's a terror."

Anita shrugged. "I'm taking a self-defence course at the Y. It'll give me a chance to practise my moves."

Nicole had not spied on her sleeping son for over two weeks. The baby monitor had remained off. It was, in fact, entirely possible that Jasper's nocturnal mumblings had ceased, which would be favourable though not exactly reassuring. If Jasper was a reincarnated terrorist, he would remain one, regardless of the language he spoke in his dreams. That night, once Jasper was in bed and she had washed the dinner dishes, she found the mini cassette recorder she had bought herself in high school, when she had been certain her destiny was to be an investigative journalist and not a paper-pusher for the government. She swapped in the flashlight batteries and clicked Play, but the tape in the machine whirred silence. The home phone rang, the number on the screen Sylvia's. She ignored it, and went downstairs.

The only light in Jasper's room was the blue glow of the digital clock on his white-noise machine. Nicole stood over her son's crib and waited for her eyes to adjust. Jasper had kicked off the blankets as usual, and was lying with his head pressed against the slats at the bottom of the crib and his feet on his pillow. The hair on his temples had dried into curls. She leaned over and felt his forehead: warm. Too warm? Her pulse quickened and she reached for his hands, then feet: cool.

She felt a fullness in her chest watching Jasper, a feeling that could be confused with love but wasn't exactly that. Or wasn't only that. There was panic there also; always, there was panic. And not just since the Arabic. Since the moment her midwife declared she could take Jasper home from the hospital. Since the hard truth of her total responsibility for this little person dug its claws in. This being the same moment she realized she had absolutely no idea what she was doing and that rather than feeling less alone, she felt more so.

It was eight-thirty. She sat on the rocker and propped her feet on the ottoman. She could barely hear Jasper's breath over the fuzz of white noise. She fell asleep.

She woke to Arabic. The clock read 10:23. Jasper's head was now on the pillow and his arms poked through the bars at the top of his crib. The blankets were balled at his feet. Nicole groped for the recorder, then fumbled for the right button. She stood and held the machine over Jasper's head, making herself remain still for a slow count of thirty. Then she clicked the recorder off and left the room. Jasper's mumbles were still audible through the door.

She climbed the stairs, then changed her mind and headed for the front door. The phone was ringing. She padded to the car in her bare feet to deposit the recorder on the passenger seat.

Back inside, she climbed the stairs, passed through the bedroom into the ensuite, flipped on the fan, turned on the tap full blast, then sat on the toilet lid and cried.

Was it unprofessional to have Anita secure a translator to decipher Jasper's sleep speech? Of course. Just as it was unprofessional to have Anita babysit her child. She would have to pay her. How much did one pay babysitters? Twelve dollars an hour? Fifteen? Or maybe she should pay Anita the same amount she earned at work. Was too much money as inappropriate as too little? Also, Nicole would have to clean. Thoroughly. She would even have to dust. Because as it was, Anita's theory about Nicole being put together would be disproved the moment she set foot inside the house.

She would start that night. It wasn't as if she'd be able to sleep.

In the kitchen rummaging for rubber gloves, she glanced at the phone. Four missed calls. She scrolled through: all from Sylvia. There was no point calling back now, her mother would be asleep. She pulled out her cell to email her a message. That the phone had died. Or that Jasper had hid it, and she'd only just discovered its hiding place.

Sylvia had a penchant for clogging Nicole's home and work email accounts with forwards that were either alarmist and a little bit racist or about kittens, all originating from her aquafit friends. There were eleven in her inbox. Also, a message with the subject line *Read ASAP*.

> Maureen Rose came to aquafit. She said while read-
> ing your tarot cards (!) you inquired about past-life
> regression. Regarding my grandson. Because I know
> you, I am quite able to follow your illogic: you believe
> your son is a reincarnated Muslim. Nonsense,
> Nicole! I can assure you the other ladies had quite a
> laugh at your expense. And at Maureen's, once she
> left. Or should I say "the French cellist's"? Thank

the lord there was a silver lining to my embarrassment. Martha, the Botoxed one married to the oph-
thalmologist (I'm sure I've told you about her), has an
exchange student from Saudi Arabia. She suggested
you record Jasper and let Karim listen. As this will
solve your imaginary dilemma, I told her I'd have a
tape next class, which is Thursday.

Nicole could just picture it, Maureen Rose arriving
at the pool in some gaudy floral swimsuit, white hair
sprouting from her armpits. Sylvia would have been
mortified when she sidled up to her in the shallow end
and began to chat. About Nicole, getting her tarot cards
read. About Nicole, seeking advice on Sylvia's grandson's
past lives. And all this within earshot of Sylvia's clique
of aquafit elite, her mother's membership in the group
already tenuous based on her class (working) and the
fact that her only offspring was an unwed mother, and
therefore not boast-worthy. To overcompensate for her
humiliation, Sylvia would have regaled the women with
a stand-up routine that centred on Nicole translating
toddler gibberish into Arabic hate speech. This would
be embarrassing if the audience hadn't been a bevy of
uptight, saggy-fleshed women in flotation belts. As it
was, Nicole was more angry than embarrassed. It wasn't
her mother's story to pass along. And she would never
have said anything to Mrs. Rose, would not even have
let her read her tarot cards, if she'd known that she'd
tattle to Sylvia.

And as for the Saudi exchange student, why would Sylvia agree to this without first consulting Nicole? Because she assumed Nicole was neurotic enough to have made a tape already. Because she knew her. And the plan had its merits: a foreign teenager translating Jasper's dream speech rather than someone Anita hired from the roster of official government translators, someone whose services Nicole might one day require for a professional purpose. Also, though she'd rather be irrational than right in this instance, she did look forward to proving Sylvia wrong. She clicked Reply and typed a one-word response:

Fine.

The next morning, after she dropped Jasper at daycare, she swung by Sylvia's house. She backed into the driveway, idled the car, then dashed to the mailbox to avoid an encounter. The moment her foot hit the front step, Sylvia appeared at the door in a fuchsia bathrobe.

"No time to say hello to your mother?"

"Hi, Mom," Nicole said. "And not really. I have an early meeting this morning." A necessary lie.

"And this is Jasper?" Sylvia asked, sticking out her hand for the recorder. "How does this little machine work?"

"Just press Play, Mom."

Sylvia pressed Play, then stuck the machine to her ear and wrinkled her forehead. "I don't hear a thing, sweetheart."

"You have to rewind it first."

The second Sylvia's finger hit the Rewind button, Nicole took off down the driveway. There was no way she was going to risk reliving last night, particularly in the company of her mother.

"Have a good day, pumpkin," Sylvia called at the top of her lungs as Nicole slammed her foot on the gas.

When she got to work, Anita was texting in her lap. When she glanced at Nicole, she dropped the phone on her chair and stood up from her desk. "You look terrible."

"Thanks, Anita."

"I mean, are you okay? Should you even be here?"

In the car mirror, Nicole had looked to herself like she always looked, just with deeper bags under her eyes. Clearly, her perception was off.

"I didn't get much sleep last night."

"I could make a coffee run. Or I've got caffeine pills." She grabbed her purse from the hook behind her and held out a dime bag of bright pink pills.

"I'll be fine," Nicole said, and reached for her office door.

"Did you make plans for Friday?"

"What's Friday?"

"Your night on the town!" Anita waggled her eyebrows at her.

"Right," Nicole said. "Yes, for sure. Thank you, Anita."

She had no plans for Friday. It was so nice of Anita to offer that Nicole hadn't wanted to tell her the truth: she had nowhere to go and no one to go there with. She was uncomfortable eating alone in public, also going solo to movies, certainly going solo to bars.

Friday evening at seven, when Anita arrived, Jasper was already asleep. Nicole had put a list of relevant phone numbers on the kitchen table. First, her cell. Next, Sylvia. Also poison control, the gas company, and the nurses' helpline. Below, she'd written a step-by-step plan for night wake-ups. Step one: ignore. Step two: wait ten minutes. Step three: call her.

The house was spotless, or at least the spots were in areas Nicole didn't expect Anita to look. Into the ensuite bathroom she had shoved all her unsorted paper stacks, the dirty laundry, a drift of broken toys. But she had scrubbed the downstairs bathroom hospital-grade clean. She had vacuumed the crumbs from the couch crevices. She had even dusted the mantel and the top of all the picture frames. The night before, she had scrubbed the downstairs floor on her hands and knees (a practice that had been encouraged by her midwife three years earlier, when Jasper was breach, and which she hadn't had the inclination to repeat since).

She had bought Nibs—which she knew Anita kept stashed in the top drawer of her desk—as well as maca-roons from the French bakery. She had bought San Pellegrino and Diet Pepsi. She had thought about wine, but Anita didn't live close by, and would that have been encouraging her to drink and drive?

She did not ask Anita if she was still smoking, but in

case she was, she had pulled a kitchen chair onto the front porch and balanced on its arm a tuna fish can filled with sand from Jasper's turtle-shaped sandbox in the backyard. She considered putting a package of wet wipes on the seat but decided this was inappropriate.

"What a gig," Anita said, settling onto the couch and grabbing a handful of Nibs from the glass dish on the coffee table. "I may have to quit my day job."

Nicole envied Anita for her sweatpants. She had opted for the black dress purchased for her aunt's funeral, heels, bare legs.

"You look amazing, Nicole. Where are you going?"

Nicole waved her hand. "Just some friends..." She would certainly be doing nothing that evening, but to complete the deception she called for a cab.

She asked the taxi driver to drop her at the dining room of the Hotel Grand Pacific, a hotel on the harbour fancy enough to have sheets with a high thread count. She ducked in, then wove her way to the front desk. It felt illicit, booking a room in a short skirt with no luggage. She could imagine what the pimpled clerk was thinking about her, and it made her shiver a little. It wasn't exactly an unpleasant feeling, though certainly it was an unfamiliar one.

Once in the room, she laid her cell on the bedside table, set the alarm to midnight and the volume to max. She hung her dress in the closet, then slipped beneath the covers. Just when she felt herself drifting off, the phone rang. It was Sylvia's number. Nicole let it go to voice mail and tried to burrow back into sleep, but the kernel of fear that had slipped in with the first ring began to expand in her chest. Maybe something was wrong with her mother. Maybe, this once, Sylvia had not called to impart all the mundane details of her day but because there was an actual emergency. She turned on the bedside light and checked the message: *Nicole, it's your mother. I just talked to Martha.* Oh God, Nicole thought, and she pressed the End button.

She lay down again, but now she was too agitated to sleep. She wanted to call Sylvia back and find out what sort of vitriol Jasper was spewing in his dreams. But she also didn't want to know. Not yet. She should enjoy this, her last night of ignorance. She drew a bath and tried to relax without getting her hair wet. She found a feel-good sports movie on pay-per-view. She took a Coke and an airplane bottle of rum from the mini-bar. And another bottle of rum. And then a gin—which she normally didn't like, but her taste buds had numbed somewhat by that point.

The phone rang every fifteen minutes. Sylvia's number every time. And every time, she felt extreme guilt for not picking up. What if this was a boy-who-cried-wolf scenario? Sylvia had initially called to reveal some terrifying details about Jasper, but perhaps now she was calling because she was choking on a Glosette, or couldn't get out of the bathtub. She remembered the TV ad from her childhood: *I've fallen . . . and I can't get up.* But she never picked up the phone. And she never checked the messages. What she wanted more than anything was to pop a sleeping pill and lie down in her own bed.

When she returned to the house just before 1 a.m., the ashtray had not been used. Anita was lying on the couch with a Dostoevsky novel in her hand. Dostoevsky!

"Your hair is appropriately disheveled," she said when she glanced up. "Have fun?"

Nicole noticed that the stack of toddler T-shirts she'd put in front of Jasper's door had been shifted somewhat to the side. "Did he wake up?"

"Well, I thought so," Anita said. "I heard him talking. But I waited a bit, like you suggested, and he stopped. I went in to check on him anyways. He was passed completely out, with both legs through the crib bars and his stuffed penguin on top of his face. You're going to think I'm crazy, but it was so warm in there, and I just felt so peaceful watching him, listening to his little snores, that I sat down on his chair and fell asleep myself. I only woke up when he started talking again. But it was just in his sleep, thank God. I wouldn't have forgiven myself if he woke up screaming because some crazy woman was asleep in his chair."

"What was he saying?" She had not considered this, the truth of her Arabic-speaking toddler being passed around the office.

Anita shrugged. "It just sounded like gibberish."

Gibberish. Was that because the Arabic was over, or because it had been gibberish all along? If Sylvia had called to say it was only gibberish, Nicole would have listened to the entire message. Then she would have slept rather than prepping for a hangover.

Nicole walked Anita to the door. She was closing it behind her when Anita turned around on the steps. "I forgot to say, your mother called. I didn't know if I was supposed to answer your phone, but it rang every five minutes and then I thought maybe it was you and you'd forgotten my cell number or something. Anyways, it was your mom. She said she had some Arabic translation for you. I wrote it down on the pad beside the phone. Which made me remember you'd said something about an Arabic translator and I totally forgot to follow up on that. Did you still want me to find one?"

Nicole shook her head. It *was* Arabic, then. Nicole had been right. But Anita didn't seem freaked out, so it couldn't have been something terrifying. Something like: *I intend to slaughter all the innocents.* Or maybe it was but Anita wasn't freaked out because she didn't know the context.

"See you Monday," Anita said.

Nicole closed the door. She walked into the kitchen. She didn't have to try to unfocus her eyes, the alcohol did that job quite nicely. She saw Anita's scrawl on the message pad. Thank God she didn't have neater handwriting. Then she flipped the pad over and went upstairs to bed.

Jasper woke at 6 a.m. Nicole's tongue felt as though it was wrapped in a tube sock. She had a second heartbeat pummelling her temples. She tried to roll over and return to sleep, but soon Jasper's screeches reached a fever pitch.

She pulled on a sweatsuit and went into his room. The second he saw her, he stood and shot his hands into the air.

"Good morning, Jasper," she said. She tried to press him to her for a second, but he wiggled out of her grasp. She smelled poop. "We have to change your diaper, kiddo."

"No," Jasper shouted, and took off for the hall.

"Whatever," Nicole muttered. She needed a coffee. And a gallon of water.

As soon as she was in the kitchen, she saw the notepad and remembered what was hidden underneath.

"Do you want cereal, Jasper?" she called through the cut-through.

"No!" he shouted. He was dragging his box of cars across the hall and into the living room.

"Do you want toast?"

"No!"

"What do you want?"

"No thing!" He flipped the box over. Cars scattered across the floor.

"Suit yourself," she said. She scooped some coffee into the press and put the kettle on to boil. Then she took a deep breath and flipped over the pad:

*8:30. Your mom. Arabic was poem. To my mother by
Mamood Darwitch (sp?)*

A poem? No, Anita must have heard wrong. She
grabbed her cell from the counter and typed the name
into Google. A new screen popped up: *showing results for
Mahmoud Darwish.* She clicked the first link and the poem
appeared.

I long for my mother's bread, it began. She sat down on
the floor and leaned her back against the cabinets, the
phone's screen inches from her face.

By the time she reached the last stanza, the tears had
started, blurring her vision: *Give me back the star maps of
childhood/ So that I/ Along with the swallows/ Can chart the
path/ Back to your waiting nest.*

She stood and went to the living room doorway. Jasper
was lining up his cars on the top of the coffee table. In a
full diaper. With an empty stomach.

"Jasper?" Nicole said.

He glanced up and held her eyes, then skidded his
gaze to the floor.

"Jasper," she repeated. Her tongue stumbled, searching for the right thing to say.

Jasper smiled. He lumbered towards her and she knelt
to eye level. He placed a hand on her knee. Then he squat-
ted to retrieve a purple Corvette, curbed against the strip
of moulding.

URSUS ARCTOS HORRIBILIS

Everyone in the Calgary ICU calls the beast Ursula. They say: Ursula has a traumatic brain injury. They say: Ursula is still in a coma. They say: We'll have to give Ursula a tracheotomy if she requires ventilation for much longer.

Kevin wants to shout: That's *not* my Ursula. But he's afraid those words might wake it, that it might leap up and whack him with the IV stand, squirt its catheter into his face. Or something. Besides, who would believe him? The nurses are always murmuring about his wife being *still very much herself*.

When there are others in the room, he calls it Ursus. Ursula would have said it was ironic, the striking similarity between her name and the name of the vile creature that destroyed her. She had seen irony in every unsettling detail. But "Ursus" puts the nurses at ease; they think Kevin is using a nickname, a term of endearment. He is lightening the mood. Only when they leave does he use

the full Latin name for the beast. Or he shortens it. As in:
you horribilis piece of shit.

Like every reckless activity they engaged in, the August
trip had been Ursula's idea. A week in the Rockies! Ursula
said. Lake Louise! Kevin had been to Lake Louise once
with a college girlfriend. In '72, before Ursula was even
born. And he had hated it. The azure water of the mor-
aine lakes hadn't, in his opinion, made up for the tourist
hordes, or the blackflies, or the disconcerting fact that
enormous man-eating animals were potentially lurking
behind every rock and tree. And though Ursula seemed
predisposed to sleep best in damp, rock-strewn environ-
ments, Kevin was not a tenter. Had simply not been born
with that gene. But as always, he gave in.

When they arrived, there was an electrified bear fence
around the campground, and charged cattle guards at the
gate to zap any paws that attempted a walk-through. That
this was necessary made Kevin even more uneasy. This,
and the warning from the teenager behind the check-in
desk: buffalo berry season. The grizzlies were out in force.
Signs blocked the trailheads threatening stiff penalties if
hikers departed in groups of fewer than four. Four people,
no more than four metres apart.

"No hiking, then," Kevin said. He tried to arrange
his face to show the disappointment he wasn't feeling.
Giant Steps, Ursula had read in the guidebook during the
drive. *Cross vast avalanche slopes for a view of the cascade. A*

strenuous, full-day hike. Ursula, though, was certain there'd be people at the trailhead. Which there were, a pair of Japanese tourists leaning against a Hertz rent-a-car. The older one wore a can of pepper spray in a holster on his belt. Also, he had on incredibly tight jeans. Kevin liked the look of those jeans. They were the pants of a man who was not interested in high-speed pursuits.

The moment Ursula stepped from the passenger side, they were upon her. "Giant Steps?" they asked, bear bells jingling.

Ursula did a full-body sweep of the men with her eyes. Then she glanced at Kevin with a smirk. "Sorry, some-place different."

He had followed her, past the bear-warning sign and onto the trail, too concerned with conserving energy to protest.

He has no photographs of Ursula. Not with him now in Calgary, and none really at all, besides ones taken when she was a kid. She spent her entire childhood posing for magazine advertisements—Shirley Temple dimples bookending a smile too big for her face. But by the time he met her, Ursula only hid behind cameras.

"Think how fragile I am," she demanded once, when Kevin had tried to coax her into the frame.

Fragile was not a word he would have used. Ursula had a ruggedness about her. She was solid, burly even, though he'd never have said so aloud. Her shoulders were broader than his. She had muscles in her legs that rippled when she walked.

"I'm probably almost hollow," she declared.

Apparently, the notion of cameras stealing souls was not exclusive to rainforest tribesmen.

If souls were vegetables, in Ursula's opinion they were onions—layers of being sealing a small and solid core. With every click of a camera's shutter, one of these layers was peeled off, seared onto film. It was the layers that fused souls to the bodies that contained them, and who knew how many one person had? Ursula wasn't hedging her bets. She was afraid of slipping away.

She burned her negatives. Every year, despite what Kevin said about keeping records, building archives, Ursula dragged her darkroom garbage can onto the deck. She melted her film into a mass of black plastic, meanwhile filling her lungs and their neighbours' open-windowed condos with noxious smoke. It was only ethical, she told Kevin. Catch and release. Of Ursula's many theories, this was one he found most endearing. He was amazed by the force of her conviction, the extent of her faithfulness.

Sometimes Kevin wishes he could give up visiting the beast, that he could simply stay away. But Ursula was who he lived for, and this is all he has left. And the shell of it *is* Ursula. Flawlessly Ursula: not even cuts, not even bruises. He sits beside her and brushes her hair off her forehead, traces her hand with his fingertips, burrows his face into the crook of her neck. Sometimes he believes he is touching his wife. But when the thing moves, when it makes even the slightest sound, he is reminded of what really exists beneath Ursula's skin, and he feels revulsion. And dread.

What else is the creature capable of? What if this Ursus rouses from its slumber and ravages the ward? Or, even worse, what if it turns against his lovely wife's body? Might it try to destroy all he has left?

Technically, they had made it all the way to Giant Steps without incident. Unless you count the scat, which looked fresh to Kevin but wasn't, according to his wife. Or the tree trunks, which only appeared clawed-up to one of them. It was on their way back from the waterfall that the grizzly appeared. Kevin and Ursula were more than four metres apart, because he was in the bushes digging a shit hole with a stick. Ursula had her camera out. And then the bear was there, right between them.

Because he was afraid of startling it into an attack, Kevin gave his directions in a whisper: "Don't make eye contact." Maybe Ursula didn't hear him. The bear was facing her, and from what he could tell, she was staring back. And then she raised her camera to her eye. She clicked the shutter. When the flash popped, the bear reared.

Its roar was solid, a sharpness that came spearing towards Ursula. Kevin did not imagine this; Ursula saw it too. She must have, because a howl surged through her throat to meet it. The sound shivered silver, suspended. Kevin was startled at first that he could see this at all, and then by the beauty of it—the round wail of his wife. But no sooner did it appear than the bear's roar pierced through. And then Ursula was thrown backwards against the ground. She was attacked, without the animal touching her. It had not charged. It did not move. And, there on the ground, neither did Ursula.

She lay still as the air shimmered. As the bear gasped.

Kevin stepped forwards, ready to rip the animal apart with his bare hands, or die trying, but the bear turned then, and the eyes he found himself looking into were not the eyes of a beast. They were frightened eyes, deep brown and beautiful eyes. Unmistakably Ursula's eyes. And though it seemed beyond possibility, he knew instantly what had happened. Ursula-bear stretched a paw to Kevin, and Kevin took it. Gripped it tightly in his hand and held it to his lips.

And then the Japanese tourists showed up with an entourage.

It's a month before Ursus is transferred to Vancouver, to St. Paul's—just blocks from their condo. And it's not until then that Kevin remembers to tell someone that Ursula is pregnant. Maybe. A year ago she had begun her whispering routine: *tick tock, tick tock*, into his ear at night. The first time she did it, his body had stiffened, and she'd responded with a deafening kiss. "Afraid of clocks, Captain Hook? Your boys not up for the challenge?" She was ten years older than Kevin's mother had been when he was born. Which was exactly six decades before. His boys likely weren't up for much, but the attempts were satisfying.

The night before Giant Steps, Ursula shook him awake at two in the morning.

"Something's happening," she said, pointing to her stomach. "You had swimmers left after all." And then she promptly fell asleep. But Kevin lay awake all night, and the later it got, the more he came to terms with his hypothetical child, the more he wanted it. He averaged the mortality rates of his relatives, trying to determine how many birthdays he'd be alive to see. Eighteen? Twenty, maybe? That Ursula would be there for everything, he took for granted.

"She's pregnant," Kevin tells the nurse at Ursula's bedside, but the woman shakes her head.

"I'm sorry, but no. No, she's not."

He had met Ursula at the Contemporary Art Gallery's auction, where his sister had dragged him citing concern for his bare white walls. Walls still pocked with nail holes from the oil paintings his first wife had taken when she left. Smeary blue-green monsters that were supposed to be seascapes. Kevin was not an art fan.

But he was a fan of Ursula immediately. Her scuffed

red shoes, the safety pin visible at the hem of her skirt. He hadn't thought her particularly pretty, but she had a captivating swagger. She was an artist, a master's student whose professor was on the board, he ascertained through eavesdropping. And she was twenty-five, exactly half his age.

Kevin had bid on her photograph, although at the time he wasn't sure what it was a photograph *of*. Hadn't known whether or not it was intentionally out of focus. The part he liked best was the promise of her name scrawled on the back. It cost him two grand.

Later, he saw her leaning over the coat-check counter, murmuring to the pimply-faced kid on the other side. The boy's hand swallowed Ursula's.

"You bought my photo," she said when she noticed him. "Does it match your couch or something?"

"Actually," Kevin replied, "it matches my toilet seat."

The pimpled boy had glared at him, but Ursula laughed. "Touché."

She told Kevin her name. She freed her hand so he could shake it. After that first time they touched, they rarely let each other go.

What was it about Kevin that appealed to Ursula? Generally, it was the heft of his wallet that solicited attention, but Ursula was unimpressed by that. In fact, in the beginning she demanded to pay half of everything, which meant dates to the Aquarium, shared sushi boats on Granville Street, pints in Gastown's seedier bars.

He'd been alive for fifty years, married for ten of them,

and for the first time he was truly in love. He slackened his hold on himself to let Ursula's dreams seep in and take root. Before her, *future* was a thought he refused to entertain, but now it meant everything. Friends asked if Ursula made him feel young again, but the truth was he felt finally and completely grown up.

The Japanese tourists may have been children of kamikaze pilots. They charged with rocks in their fists. Kevin could feel Ursula pulling away, so he gripped her paw tighter. A rock bounced off her flank and hit him in the stomach.

"Stop," Kevin called.

But they didn't stop. Only flung more, and harder, and then the one with the jeans launched himself at Kevin's back. Kevin lost hold of his bear-wife and hit the ground hard. He tried to claw his way back up, but the air was a cloud of cayenne pepper. His eyes burned. He couldn't see a thing.

"The bear," Kevin coughed, and the Japanese tourists waved their hands, motioning that it was far away. A woman hovered her cheek inches above Ursula's mouth, listening for breath.

Kevin tried to stand, to set out in search of his bear-wife, but a hefty man caught him from behind and pressed him still. "Shhh," the man said, taking off his sweater and draping it over Kevin's shoulders. "Shhh." Kevin closed his eyes. Maybe, when he opened them, he'd be back in the tent. Maybe none of this was real.

"Don't fear of bear," whispered a woman with a thick German accent. "Bear is gone."

After three months in St. Paul's, there is a change. Ursus is in a private room on the third floor. It is breathing without a ventilator. But the change Kevin feels is one of tone, of mood. He can't put his finger on it exactly; one day the sight of Ursus angers him as much as always, but the next day in the beast's presence he remains strangely calm. He feels as though someone is sitting with him the entire visit, murmuring gentle words in a register he can sense but cannot hear. In fact, twice he gets up from his chair and inspects the room and the corridor outside.

When he is confident that he and Ursus are alone, he becomes, for a moment, desperately hopeful about the recovery of his wife. Could she be trapped inside this shell of herself, cohabiting with the creature? But Ursula had been a force, a shriek of vibrancy. Standing in the hallway in front of their apartment, Kevin always knew if Ursula was inside by her gravitational pull. It formed tides in his blood.

He doesn't feel her now but he feels something—something both new and hauntingly familiar. Like he's come home to a place his memory had erased.

He had forgotten to cancel the newspapers. When Ursula was transferred to the ICU at St. Paul's, he went back to the condo and found a pile of them in the hall beside the door. The attack was on the front cover of one, and this: young sow located near scene and humanely destroyed.

How do you mourn someone who everyone else thinks is still alive? Ursula's parents flew to Vancouver to hold a month-long vigil at the hospital. Her friends and co-workers ensured a constant collection of bedside bouquets. Yet there was no point to any of this; Ursula was gone.

Kevin began to pack her things, but the half-full boxes reminded him of when Ursula first moved into the apartment. The elation he felt then, and the terror. He shut the boxes in the bedroom, leaving on the lamp beside the bed. Sometimes at night he lay on the couch staring at the thread of light beneath the bedroom door, pretending Ursula was inside. And then the lamp burned out.

There comes a day when Kevin realizes he is more content in the hospital room than anywhere else. Is this disloyalty to his wife? The nurses are pleased because now, when they enter the room, they come upon Kevin talking, something they have always maintained might help. Except he's not talking to Ursus, or even Ursula; he's talking to whoever else is contained within those four walls.

Deep in the pit of himself, he knows what the presence is. But he won't mention it aloud to anyone. As Kevin's secret, the presence is possible. But breathed into daylight, he's afraid the truth of it won't hold up.

In mid-March he is sitting with Ursus, reading the *Sun*, when the night nurse touches his shoulder.

"Kevin?"

He turns, and she looks quickly away. The flush in her cheeks deepens, spreads to her ears, down her neck.

"Kevin, have you been intimate with your wife?"

"Ever?" he asks.

"I was bathing her, Kevin, and I noticed some changes. We did a test. Kevin?" This time she finds his eyes. "Ursula is pregnant."

"How long?" he asks. And then he holds his breath, waiting for the answer that would make everything better, would make everything make sense.

"Four months," the nurse says.

"Four months," Kevin repeats. It has been seven since the attack. His body feels charged, electric.

When he and Ursus first got back to Vancouver, Kevin had worked his way through all the books on Ursula's shelves. Books by Benjamin, Foucault, and Barthes. A book on bears. In the bear book he read about blastocysts, fertilized eggs that develop only into minuscule embryos, then float in the uterus for several months. Float until the sow is denned for winter and her body determines whether she is fit to birth young. At which point it either implants in the uterus, and a fetus develops, or it doesn't; it is simply reabsorbed. *Giving the bear*, the book said, *more control over her reproduction than almost any other animal.*

Not complete control, Kevin thinks now. He imagines Ursus discovering life in Ursula's body, and raging at having to share its hijacked home with a human child. For three months Ursus had ruled, forcing the baby to hover aimlessly in Ursula's womb. Trying, likely, to destroy it, just as it ensured the destruction of his wife. And then Ursus let its guard down and the baby seized the opportunity.

The baby grabbed on to Ursula's uterus, its cells multiplying, clustering into smooth and perfect fetal flesh. The tenacity this baby had! The doggedness! These things it had inherited from Ursula, its mother.

But that the baby had withstood the wait, that it endured—this the baby had learned from days spent with Kevin. It was proof the child was his.

⚜ DOUBLE DUTCH

The last time I visited them in Bel Air, he didn't know me. Nancy led me to the leather armchair he was sitting in, feet propped on the coffee table, a rolled tube of magazine clutched in both fists.

"Ronnie." She bent so her face was level with his, her lips almost brushing his ear. "Ronnie, Noah has come to see you."

When he looked up, I smiled. After an instant his lips mimicked mine, but then he lifted his hand to his mouth and began to chew at the raw skin around his thumbnail. Nance patted his knee twice quickly and he pulled his thumb away, then unfurled the magazine and flattened it against his leg. It was the last week's copy of the *TV Guide*, the Raiders posed on the cover.

A gauzy cashmere sweater was draped over the ottoman. I sat beside it, my fingers weaving through the sleeve. "You been watching some football, Dutch?" I asked.

He nodded, but his eyes didn't rise from his lap.

"Who do you figure will take the Super Bowl?"

"I've always been a fan of the Fighting Irish," he said. His eyes darted between me and the *TV Guide*, but his voice was clear and unwavering. It was like he was reciting his lines but wasn't sure if he'd gotten them exactly right. Had he been a fan of Notre Dame? I couldn't remember.

"The Fighting Irish," he repeated. His face brightened and he nodded. "I knew a fellow, the Gipper. He used to play for them."

Nancy was leaning against the door frame, her back to me. Her shoulders rose and fell with her breath.

"George Gipp, isn't that right, Dutch?" I asked. "He was a real hero."

His hands still stroked the magazine, but he was no longer looking at it. He gazed upwards. "I'm not a hero, but I saved some lives."

"Really," I said. "That's a story I'd love to hear." I hated the way I spoke to him, my tongue's movements slow and deliberate, tasting every perfect syllable. Like I was talking to an especially dim child.

"I swam." Reagan squinted at the wooden beam that ran across the ceiling. I imagined his memories projected there, a cracked and dust-coated film reel clicking through the frames. "There was a river in town. I saved a child. His mother kissed me. On my lips in front of her husband. There were others. I think there was more than one."

"That's right," I said. "You saved seventy-seven lives in seven summers."

"Seventy-seven." His skin was pallid, but his eyes shone. If I looked hard, I could almost see in them the man I had known, and the proud teenager he must have been, lifeguarding at Rock River. "I saved them all. I was a swimmer." His face crumpled suddenly. "Mommy," he called. And when Nance hurried towards him, Reagan held out both arms to her, then swallowed her hands with one of his mitt-sized fists. "Mommy," he repeated. He leaned into her, but his eyes were on me.

"It's always nice when Noah visits us, isn't it, Ronnie?" Nance pulled one hand free and patted Reagan's thigh. "We always enjoy Noah's visits, don't we?" She nodded as she spoke, and soon Reagan's head was bobbing along with hers.

It was November 1994, almost fourteen years to the day since I'd been granted a role in Reagan's life. And in Nancy's. But there would only be visits now. The more he faded, the more certain it seemed that I would be erased along with him.

By that November, I hadn't watched *Knute Rockne* in years; I'd left my copy in my brother Bill's trailer when I went to Washington. But some nights the film still played in my head when I slept. I'd wake with the video-cover image seared across my eyelids: Reagan with his hands on his hips, filling the frame, his name in bold right under Pat O'Brien's. Not bad for a bit part. And it *was* a bit part. The movie was 138 minutes. The Gipper walked onto the field in minute 34 and died in minute 46. And everything on that football field—a good half of those twelve minutes—wasn't even him.

Reagan always claimed he had pitched the Rockne film then had to fight for a role. With his sharp face and dark eyes, he didn't look the part of the coach: a middle-aged Norwegian. And so he was cast as George Gipp, hotshot halfback. Reagan had played football in school, and this gave him a leg up on the others who read for the part; he could kick, pass, and tackle, no need to hire an extra. But the morning shooting began, he was roughing with O'Brien and sprained an ankle. It swelled to the size of his thigh. There was no chance he'd be able to boot the ball; he could barely tie his cleat.

Bill warmed the bench for the Fighting Irish in 1939, and he and a handful of his teammates were chosen to throw the ball around with Reagan onscreen. My father gave me a day off from the grocery to watch them. Ruth and I were cuddled on the bleachers when the ball landed two rows over. I kicked it back.

On the grass beside Reagan, Bill pointed me out, his older brother Noah. "Folks even say he looks like you." *Like a goddamn mirror*, Reagan said, after he'd shouted me down to see for himself. Ten minutes later, I was suited up.

George Gipp walks onto the screen tossing a baseball. The pigskin arcs his way and he catches it and steps backwards. The camera shifts to a back view; the Gipper punts and the ball flies over the bleachers. "Look at that ball travel—must have gas in it," Rockne says. The kick was mine. That and all that came next: another punt, some banter with O'Brien—and here I tried out Reagan's honey-over-gravel voice, his blank-faced stare. Watch closely and you'll see the only differences: the hips suddenly narrow, the smaller ears.

The truth of the ankle appears in minute twelve of the Gipper's screen time. He's in the hospital bed, Reagan himself this time. He's smiling, being brave for the coach—but there's a grimace beneath. I hate to say it, but that's the quality of acting Reagan couldn't pull off— two emotions expressed at once. He managed because the grimace was real. And that famous line: "Ask them to go in and give all they've got... win just one for the Gipper," delivered like he was clenching his teeth against the pain. He was.

Maybe I could have made a go at show business. Folks said Reagan's looks were what got him places, and in that department I was his equal. Plus, I wasn't a bad actor. Certainly made a career of it in my later years. But there was the war, and it changed things. The Japs taking over the airwaves in the Philippines, playing Crosby's "Waiting for Ships That Never Come In" after the fall of Singapore, and you're roasting rats and iguanas on a fire because that's all that's left for food. Marching over the swollen, heat-blackened bodies of your buddies, led by the man who stole your watch and the photographs you held to your heart since you left home. A month of rolling darkness on a ship to Korea. A submarine attack and you trampled by a screaming mob, bodies hitting the hull like birds against the glass walls of office towers. Three and a half years in a chicken coop in Manchuria, shitting yourself from dysentery, dead to everyone you ever knew. Then home at under a hundred pounds, the two people you missed most having filled the empty places in their lives with each other. A wailing baby in your girl's arms, your brother by her side. That changes things. That changes everything. But that wasn't even the beginning.

November 4, 1980.

Yellow Point, BC, in November is wet layers of green and grey. I'd tied a tarp over the roof of the coop so the hens were dry, but the ground was mud and the rooster had come outside to strut in it. By the time the clock struck ten, Ruth still hadn't arrived to collect the eggs, so I did it myself. I managed to keep one foot planted in the yard while I lunged through the doorway and rifled around in the straw, all the while the hens performing a squawking, feather-flapping assault against my arm. I hoped to God no one would catch me in the middle of this routine; I knew what I looked like. But no matter how much sense I tried to talk myself into, every time I stepped foot inside, I had visions of some SOB in a threadbare US Marine uniform frozen stiff in the corner.

Ruth came half an hour later, while I was washing the dishes. I could hear her whistling before I saw her through the kitchen window, newly permed hair tied back with a clear plastic kerchief and those red rubber boots that were hand-me-downs from her grandson. She ducked into the coop, then came out again empty-handed and made a beeline for my door.

"Sorry I wasn't here earlier," she said when I opened it. "I was—"

"I'm fine to do it myself." I pointed to the carton on the table: six eggs, plus two cups of empty shells that had been my breakfast.

"Sure," she said. "I know that." But she didn't move from my step.

"Where's Bill?"

"Oh." She waved her hand like she was dusting the air between us. "I expect he's off entertaining himself somehow."

You know, Bill had said to me a year after I got back from Manchuria, Ruth fit to burst with their second, *I wouldn't blame you if you were still in love with her, if you wanted her back*. It was true that in those first few months I felt a jolt like a sucker punch in my gut every time I laid eyes on her, but it wasn't love anymore. I longed for the girl I had made her into: the one who nagged me into surviving those years I was away—had me digging through frozen dirt for bugs and roots and doing jumping jacks when it would have been easiest to let the cold cover me like a blanket. But that wasn't Ruth. Ruth's voice was soft and always on the verge of tears: when the baby was colicky, when the dinner burned, and every time she said my name. I didn't think I could stand to hold something so easily broken, to be responsible for something as fragile as a woman's happiness. It was later that year that Bill got a job in Canada. They both asked me to move up there with them. But whether their request was made out of guilt or love, it didn't matter; at that time I needed to be on my own.

When I stepped back from the doorway, Ruth came right in without being asked. Walked to the couch and picked up the stack of videos I'd left beside the VCR from the night before: *The Big Heat* and a couple of Hitchcocks. "Noah, do you ever watch the Reagan movies?" She was staring at the cover of *Rear Window*, tracing her finger around Jimmy Stewart's face. "I still watch *Knute Rockne*. Bill says he's sick of it, but I watch it sometimes when I'm alone. It gets me wondering."

"Do you think he'll win tonight?" I asked, taking the stack of videos from her and placing the egg carton in her hands.

She looked at me for a moment too long, then shrugged. "If you get lonely, you know where to find us."

That evening, I turned on the TV to see if I could get the election coverage, but even the usual channels were staticky with the rain. I dug through the half-dozen boxes on the bedroom floor—what was left of my South Bend movie collection—and stuck *Knute Rockne* in the VCR instead.

By the time the Gipper died, I wasn't paying any attention to the screen. I had the closet open and was lining up the food cans, counting and recounting. Outside, the bent forks Bill and Ruth's grandkids had hung in the apple tree chimed in the wind. My mind kept circling the same question: how was it that paths that had once converged could lead to such distant places — one man starring in films and running for president and the other spending half a lifetime changing reels in a movie theatre and ending up in a trailer he doesn't own beside a chicken coop he can't bear to enter? When Rockne's plane went down, I switched off the set, made myself a cup of tea, and lay down to sleep.

I woke at four in the morning to someone pounding the door, the darkness split by a beam of light through the front curtains. I stopped short of screaming, bracing myself for the blows before the old dreams slipped off. And then my mind flew to Bill and Ruth, and something being wrong with one or the other of them. But when I opened the door, it was to two men I didn't recognize, clean-shaven and suited. There was a black van by the coop, high beams on.

"Noah Driscoll?"

The bigger of the two did the talking. He pushed his way through the door and stood leaning against the stove. The slight one followed him in.

"Ronald Reagan has requested a meeting with you."

My first thought: he must have done it, then, got himself elected. It seemed strange to think that the next president would be a man I had met, a man people said I resembled. My next thought: I had nothing to offer Reagan, surely. What would he want with me?

Here's a story for you: The famous Shawnee leader Tecumseh suffered defeat at the hands of William Henry Harrison in 1811, then died in 1813 fighting troops Harrison led. His brother, a medicine man, cursed Harrison and every fifth president that followed him — all men elected or re-elected in a "zero year." This is called Tecumseh's Curse.

In 1840, Harrison was elected. He died of pneumonia one month after his inauguration.

In 1860, Abe Lincoln was elected. He was assassinated during his second term, while attending a play.

In 1880, James A. Garfield was elected, and the next year he was shot in the back in a railroad station waiting room. He died eighty days later, of complications related to a bullet that his doctors couldn't find.

In 1900, William McKinley was re-elected. The following September he was shot while shaking hands with a crowd in Buffalo. He died of gangrene.

In 1920, Warren Harding was elected. Three years later he died of a stroke, a heart attack, or food poisoning at a San Francisco hotel. (His wife, who some suspected was part of a plot against him, would not grant permission for an autopsy.)

In 1940, FDR was elected for a third term. At the beginning of his fourth term, he suffered a fatal brain hemorrhage while sitting for a portrait.

In 1960, JFK was elected. He was assassinated by Lee Harvey Oswald in 1963.

In 1980, it was Reagan's turn at the helm of the country.

I didn't know anything about Tecumseh's Curse when the CIA appeared on my step; it was Nance, with her belief in all things mystical, who later filled me in on that. But I knew that more than a couple punts of a pigskin would be required of me if I agreed to go with them.

"I can't," I said. "No." It wasn't that I had much of a life in Yellow Point. No job except for an egg stand on the side of the road and the occasional wood chopping for the neighbours. No friends but Bill and Ruth. I had the things I wanted, though: space and quiet. The men began to pack for me anyway.

When they opened the closet to the stacks of cans, the skinny one laughed out loud. "You believe in Armageddon, Mr. Driscoll?" he asked.

He was so young and smug. *I've seen it*, I thought of replying, but I didn't say a word.

I sat at the table and wrote a letter to my brother and his wife. I told them the truth: five years was a long time to take advantage of their hospitality. And it was easier to disappear than to say goodbye. And then I lied: as soon as I found some place to call home for a while, I'd let them know, and I would always keep in touch. It was still dark when I crossed the yard to put the letter in the mailbox, but the light in their front room was on and I could see the silhouette of the tabby through the blinds. Bill was probably awake as well, but I turned away before I had a chance to see him. By the afternoon, I was in Bel Air.

When we arrived at Reagan's home, it was another agent who opened the door. Nancy was in the dining room, facing the window, and my first sight of her was the smooth arc of her neck.

"It is striking, the resemblance," she said when she turned. She didn't acknowledge me, only addressed the man who had shown me in. "Though his weight is wrong, and something will have to be done with his hair. And of course, Ronnie carries himself differently." Folded in her lap, her hands were as small as a child's.

"Comportment can be learned," the agent said.

"Yes, I suppose that's true." She shifted her attention to me then. "Mr. Driscoll, I expect you understand the importance of this position, and the valuable role you will play in the president's security. If you'll take a seat, I'd prefer to speak to you myself about our expectations before Ronnie joins us."

She was brisk, all business. Everything about her was perfectly in place, perfectly considered, from her clothes and makeup to the words she spoke and the smile that she gave only with her lips.

Before I say more, there are things I need to set straight about Nancy. I won't deny all the rumours: the redecorating expenses, for example—new china, blinds, and carpeting for the White House while Reagan was busy slashing budgets elsewhere. But before you judge, you should have the facts. Nancy is a lady, so she never let the world in on the reason for this: Rosalynn Carter may well have been a sweet woman, but she wasn't a tidy one. The White House was a disaster when we moved in.

In fact, there was something to all the reports about Nancy. But those particles of truth were exaggerated, expanded, fabricated into stories for newspapers that thrived by bulldozing reputations. For instance, Nancy probably did rifle through Patti's drawers and listen in on her phone conversations. If she were my daughter, I'd have done the same. But if you knew Nancy, you'd know she never hit her. And you'd know the stories about pill popping were also lies. Sure, I saw her take pills—for headaches, and nerves, and sometimes for sleep. Do you think being Reagan's wife would be easy? The stepkids with chips the size of dinner plates on their shoulders, a ballet dancer for a son, a daughter who slept with half of California. Nancy suffered through all this with dignity. But she did suffer. I knew that the second I looked in her eyes that day in Bel Air.

"Mr. Driscoll?" Nance repeated. Her voice was flat, but her hands were clenched and in her chin I saw the quiver before tears.

I had rehearsed it the entire flight—my refusal—but standing face to face with Nancy Reagan, I couldn't get the words out of my mouth.

I agreed to stand by Reagan's side, or—more accurately— in his place, as frequently as was required for his first one hundred days in office. On day 101, my contract would be renegotiated. It wouldn't be renewed; I was certain. What did I know about acting? I had played so few roles in my life: a projectionist after the war and then a quarter-century later—when the theatre burned down—a hermit in the woods. I'd moved to Canada because in almost thirty years Bill and Ruth had not retracted their invitation, and because I had no place else to go. Once there, I'd gone on living life the way I always had: through books and movies. Alone. At sixty-six, I was too old for changes.

Reagan was older by three years. He was also more determined. I had just under three months to train for the part, and he decided to be my coach. Two days after my arrival, he brought a pile of clothes to the guest room for a dress rehearsal. He watched me change, inspecting my body for disparities and pointing out the ones he found: the cluster of moles on my back, my crooked toe, my war wounds—the angry white scars that jagged up my left leg. When I had fixed the knot on my tie, he crossed the room and stood directly in front of me, mimicking my posture, the expression on my face. *Like a goddamn mirror*, he said. He was chuckling when he reached out to smooth my lapel. And then he paraded me into the living room, where Nancy was sitting on the couch reading a presidential profile in *Life* magazine.

"Be me," Reagan instructed, flopping down beside his wife, crossing his arms over his chest. Nancy put her magazine on her lap.

I cleared my throat.

With my hands balled in fists, I took a step towards them. "It's about time we taught the welfare bums about the benefits of an honest day's work. About putting their hands to use, not sticking them in the pockets of the taxpayers." It was something he'd said the previous afternoon.

Nancy drew in her breath sharply.

Reagan laughed, then shook his head. He stood up and loosened his tie, ran a hand through his hair. "Just get up off the ground, that's all I ask." There was a pained expression on his face. His voice was hoarse. "Get up there with that lady that's up on top of this Capitol dome, that lady that stands for liberty. Take a look at this country through her eyes if you really want to see something."

It was a quote from a movie I'd watched hundreds of times. *"Mr. Smith Goes to Washington,"* I said.

"That's the ticket." Reagan slapped me on my back before settling onto the couch. "Try again."

Did he want me to be him or Jimmy Stewart? I looked at him for clues, but his eyes were glazed.

"Ronald Reagan is the American Everyman," Nancy murmured. She was smiling slightly, like the two of us were sharing a secret behind her husband's back.

The American Everyman. I stood taller and squared my shoulders. "We can't do away with government," I said. "So instead we must make it work. We should make it work *with* us. It should stand at our side and not ride on our backs..."

I glanced up. Nancy had her head cocked to the side, still watching me. Reagan was beaming.

"That's me," he said. "Isn't it, Mommy?"

"Yes," Nancy said, her eyes locked to mine. "This will work."

There was a chemistry with Nancy. Maybe now she'd deny it, but it seemed to me it went deeper than my resemblance to her husband. That first time I became Ronald Reagan, I watched Nancy watching me and I thought about the bed she shared. I thought about the way Reagan draped his body around hers even when there were others in their presence. The way she looked at him. Those were the scenes I wanted to rehearse.

"Do you have much interest in politics, Noah?" Nancy asked.

I shook my head. "I've never had much of an opinion on the subject, Mrs. Reagan."

"That's good," Reagan said. "We're the salesmen. We don't come up with the ideas—we go out there and sell them."

By the time Reagan was inaugurated, my hair was long enough to slick into a pompadour. I'd put on ten pounds. And I hadn't called Bill and Ruth once. I missed things: Bill's laughter, how easily Ruth and I shared silences, the sound of rain on the trailer's roof. But when I was Reagan, I forgot that I had ever been anyone else. And it felt good, that forgetting. Noah Driscoll may have been hopeless, but Ronald Reagan was his antithesis. He was powerful and commanding. He was loved. And in those first two months, I was Reagan almost always; Nancy insisted on the practice.

I watched the inauguration on a television set in a Washington hotel, two Secret Service men standing at the door. First Reagan swearing his oath, wearing the silver tie I had suggested. Then standing beside Nancy for the inauguration parade, hands clasped over his head like he'd flattened an opponent in the boxing ring. And meanwhile, Iran released fifty-two American hostages, the synchronicity of these events staged in advance. It was the perfect prelude to the presidency, and I was counting the moments until I stepped into my role. But being president suited Reagan just as much as being Reagan suited me. Whenever it was suggested I take his place, he claimed there was no need. His security was not threatened; why not save me for something else? And so I was stuck as Noah Driscoll, except I was Noah Driscoll caged in the White House. I stayed in my room on the second floor. I watched movies and counted cans of food. I had nightmares. And I lasted exactly sixty-eight days before I started writing my letter of resignation. I was on my third draft when Nancy knocked at my door.

I stood to let her in, leaving the letter on the desk. Sometimes I wonder if all that happened next was meant to make me stay, intended to solicit commitment. Some say that Nance would stop at nothing to get her way. But I prefer to believe she never doubted my loyalty. Never suspected a thing.

She perched on the edge of the bed and the sidelight

caught her kneecap, then she sighed. "Noah?" she said.

Although her presence always caused a flood of words to rise inside me, I didn't dare speak. She caught my eye and smiled, so sudden and unrehearsed that I lost hold of myself. There was a blood surge to my crotch, and I did the only thing I could think of: I cupped Nancy's hand in mine and raised her wrist to my mouth.

I know you won't believe me, but maybe you can believe this: Cassiopeia of freckles on her left shoulder blade, a scar white as teeth on her ankle, tea-stained splash on the inside of her right thigh, nipples the colour of a bruised peach.

Her body was light as sparrow bones, so that as she lay on top of me I half expected the breeze from the ceiling fan to lift her, feathers pushing from her arms as she swooped away. But it wasn't the wind that carried her. It was the Secret Service men: opening the door to my lips on Nancy's breast. Their stony-faced expressions as they announced that Reagan was in the hospital. That while my mouth had sucked and burrowed, devouring all it could of his wife, the president was frothing blood, a bullet lodged in his lung.

When Nancy left with the Secret Service men, I turned on the television in my room. The announcer claimed that the president was unharmed, then that the president was hit, then that Brady the press secretary was dead, then only injured. My first thoughts were selfish: If Reagan died, would Nancy still need me, or would my time with her be over? Would I get what I had wished for only hours earlier, before the sight of a bare leg changed everything? And then my next thought: if Reagan died, would it be possible for me to take his place?

I opened my closet and started to count my cans of food — tilting each one so the labels were perfectly centred. I did it three times over, letting the act quiet the noise in my head. It was only when I was finished that I realized the target should have been me. That's what I was there for. Hinckley with his *Taxi Driver* fantasies, his bullets of longing for Jodie Foster, should have fired into my chest. I felt the threat then, and yet Nancy's smell was still on my hands, her taste still on my lips.

Nance wanted to spend the night in the hospital, but the Secret Service brought her home, the advisers suggesting it would send a message that Reagan was strong if Nancy was photographed abandoning the bedside vigil. I couldn't leave my room when she arrived because her children were with her, but she came just before dawn. She let herself in and sat where she had earlier that day.

"I need you to promise you'll stay." She'd been crying. The makeup smears beneath her eyes looked like bruises. And I wasn't foolish enough to believe her intentions were for anything but a false target.

I hosted state dinners. I gave speeches and attended press conferences. For Reagan, the bullet had sheered the glamour off, but my stepping in was more on Nancy's insistence. She wanted to keep me practised at the role.

And though she'd never give me so much as a kiss again, I stayed. I stayed because Nancy Reagan wanted me to.

By the second year of the presidency, all Reagan could talk about were the Soviets. The "evil empire" that was targeting America in general, and him specifically. As president of the Screen Actors Guild, he had defeated the Communist conspiracy to take over Hollywood. As president of the most powerful nation on earth, he was charged with battling a global threat.

"I'll send you to the NORAD base," he said once, when I failed to be sufficiently terrified by his predictions. We were sitting in the Oval Office drinking Cokes, sifting through his piles of mail. Reagan spent more time reading his letters than he did reading policy briefs. And so did I.

"In Cheyenne Mountain," he clarified, though I'd heard the story before. It was one of his favourites. That Douglas Morrow had secured him the invitation. That Reagan had toured the vast underground city, winding his way through a maze of rooms and corridors carved deep into the granite. And that finally he'd stepped through a steel door three feet thick and into the command centre. The room like something out of a movie set: a screen showing a multi-storey US map on the far wall. In front, beside panels of switches and flashing lights, a sea of young men monitoring the skies.

"They track everything in space," he said. "They're even tracking—"

A glove lost by an astronaut, I mouthed along with him.

"But that's all they *can* do. They can track a Soviet missile from its launch pad to the moment it strikes the White House, but they can't stop it."

"It doesn't make sense," I said. "They can do all that, but they can't defend us?"

"That's what I said." Reagan struck the table with his fist.

"If scientists can invent nuclear bombs, you'd think they could come up with something. A defensive weapon that will make all nuclear weapons obsolete," I added, knowing he would get the reference.

"Torn Curtain," Reagan murmured. He closed his eyes. "Like a roof," he said after a moment. "A roof to keep out the missiles."

"A shield," I said.

"Making nuclear weapons obsolete." He spoke the words like he was tasting them, then pulled an index card from his shirt pocket. "Hand me a pen."

Something Reagan did admire about the Communists was that from the beginning they too had hired men to stand in their places. A double lived with Stalin for months to give Beria and his gang another target to go after. Stalin didn't attend meetings himself that entire time, until his decoy took ill from some warfarin-infused vodka. Hours later, old Joe was given a taste of the same medicine.

But it wasn't just the Communists. Hess and Himmler

almost got off scot-free after WWII, their doubles captured in their places. Hitler's double surfaced before
him too, though his had been murdered and burned up.
Unfortunate for him that the fire didn't do a better number on the decoy's jaw; if it hadn't been for the discrepancy
in dental records, no one would have been the wiser. The
CIA always claimed that if the Führer had known what
was coming his way, he *would* have blown his brains out
in his bunker.

Americans are more secretive about their decoys, and
except for Henry Kissinger with his bouts of stage fright,
I never heard of a politician who employed one. The CIA
dabbled in them from time to time, but if you were to see
the decoyed and his decoy side by side, ten times out of
ten you'd be able to spot the fake immediately.

Now Reagan and I weren't 100 percent identical
either, but the features we didn't share were the ones
nobody paid attention to anyways. For instance, if we
were together, you could see that he had larger feet and
thinner fingers, and I had a slightly sharper chin, but it
seemed to be impossible for most people, including the
ones who knew both of us—a handful of Reagan staffers
and the Secret Service—to sort the real president from
his counterfeit.

You likely saw the news clips of Reagan's summit meetings with Gorbachev. Geneva and Reykjavik, Washington
and Moscow. Likely you even watched a clip of Reagan
and Mikhail in Iceland played back to back with their
little tête-à-tête in the USSR. And I'm sure you weren't

thinking that these were two different Reagans you were viewing. But they were. I went to the first two summits in Reagan's place. Nancy said she had a bad feeling about Geneva, a worse feeling about Reykjavik, the result of less than favourable astrological forecasts. Maybe she did. But I know that some of Reagan's advisers had also expressed concerns about the commander-in-chief. What he might do if it came down to him and Mikhail in a room together. Reagan had a joke he liked. *How do you tell a Communist? Well, it's someone who reads Marx and Lenin. And how do you tell an anti-Communist? It's someone who understands Marx and Lenin.* He'd told it to a pair of Maoist diplomats. I know everyone expected he'd open his mouth around Gorbachev and say something just as bad.

It was November 1985 when we went to Geneva. I hadn't been alone with Nancy since I flew with her to Germany earlier that year, since she'd clutched my arm in Bergen-Belsen, buried her face in my shoulder after glancing at some blown-up photos of tangled corpses. During the war, I'd seen things just as bad, but Reagan hadn't. He'd stayed on US soil starring in instructional videos. And so I'd made a display of my horror. And I'd held on to Nancy just as tight.

But Switzerland was a bigger deal than Germany had been, and the administration was nervous. They called for a news blackout. If I slipped up, they wanted to ensure the world wouldn't start asking questions. The day before Mikhail arrived, Nancy and I sat in the pool house at Fleur d'Eau for a test run. There were aides there, and so I was

Ronald Reagan. I stared into her eyes; I gripped her hand; she offered me encouragement. But that night, like every other, there was a wall dividing our beds.

Just as planned, Mikhail and I did sit in that pool house by the lakeside, the fire roaring. We went alone, except for the interpreters. He hammered me about reviving the B-1 bomber program that Carter had cancelled, and about Star Wars, the space shield I had inspired myself. And I read from my talking points, typed out on three-by-five cards, just as Reagan always did: We needed an acceleration of arms talks. We should meet again. And then I told him stories about Hollywood.

"Nuclear war will never be won," he said to me the final morning through his translator. "It should never be fought."

"You know," I answered, "if aliens from outer space invaded earth, America and the Soviet Union would soon forget their national differences and get together as human beings."

He shook my hand. Not even the press could deny the brilliance of my performance.

Reagan didn't actually sit down with a Soviet until Gorbachev came to Washington. By then, the USSR had already announced glasnost and perestroika, and Reagan's "Tear down this wall" speech in East Berlin had faded in their memories. In other words, the possible consequences were much less dire.

To tell you the truth about the Soviets, I felt no enmity towards them. Not like Reagan did. After all, all those years ago it was the Russians who had entered Mukden from the Gobi Desert, captured the Japanese, and loaded them onto trucks and trains. Who knows what they did with them next. Once, I saw a Russian soldier order three Japs to unload supplies from his truck. When they were finished, he lined them up against the fence and put a bullet into each of their heads. Whenever I saw Mikhail, that's what I thought of: liberation.

No one I met while I was Ronald Reagan had a moment's suspicion of my true identity — except one person. Nancy I could never fool. A couple months after the assassination attempt, Reagan and I were in the Oval Office drinking sodas and going through the notes I'd taken during a meeting with a pair of South American diplomats. There had been a horse race on satellite that afternoon, and Reagan had a bet riding on the outcome, so he'd stayed in my room to watch.

"Terrific, Noah," he said after I told him how I'd entertained the men with Hollywood stories I'd invented on the spot: Bogart's affair with Bette Davis, Brando's pantyhose collection, Olivia de Havilland's fierce halitosis. "Let's try something." And then he had his finger on the intercom, asking for Nancy to be sent to the room. "Shh," he said when we heard the knock on the door. He knelt beside me and tucked himself under the desk.

"Mommy," I said when Nancy entered. It felt wrong to use that word on her, but Reagan had a grip on my ankle and I could tell I was supposed to play along.

"Hello, Ronnie," she said. "How were the horse races?"

"Oh," I said. "Well, uh—"

"I know you were watching them." She sat down on the chair beside the desk, placing the memo pad Reagan had left there on her lap. She took a pen from the coffee table and started to write something in the margin.

"Not fair," she said without looking up. "To make that poor man do everything for you."

"He doesn't mind."

"Maybe," she said. "I suppose there are some things he'd be happy to take on himself." She placed the pad on the corner of the desk and stood up, then leaned over until her face was inches from mine. She reached out one slender finger and brushed something from the corner of my mouth. My hand raced up to meet hers before I thought about what I was doing. And then Reagan sprang up from the floor.

"Ha," he shouted. "Gotcha!"

"Oh, what a clever joke," Nancy said. She pulled her hand from mine and turned to Reagan, cupped his face, and squeezed his cheeks like he was a child. He was still sputtering with laughter when she let go. I slid the memo pad towards me and read my name in Nancy's scrawl across the top. She saw me looking and ripped the sheet off, crumpled it in her fist, and tossed it in the wastebasket without Reagan noticing.

Reagan and I restaged the trick plenty of times. He would call Nancy into the Oval Office, me hiding out of sight. He'd call her in five minutes later and I'd be in his place—same suit, same mug of coffee in my hand.

"Hello, Noah," she'd always say, never missing a beat. "What have you done with Ronnie?"

Maybe you think I was glad she knew me well enough to see me as someone separate, but I got more pleasure from being a stand-in—her calling me Ronnie in front of visitors, in front of the press—than I ever got from her using my name. It was only when I was Reagan that I could almost convince myself I was hers.

I lived in the White House for eight years—spent most of my time in the second-floor suite where only Reagan and Nance went, and the staffers who knew about me. It got dull there, and sometimes a man needs to wander: get some fresh air, see an open sky. Some say that truly great actors can convince themselves they are the character they're playing, and I did that. Still, I tried to dodge all political conversation when I wandered the halls—nodding and wrinkling my forehead if I was cornered, then walking away with my head still shaking, as if I were giving it all some thought. The charade wasn't always successful. Some chose to follow at my heels until they were satisfied with my response. In that way, I learned about a lot of stuff I wanted nothing to do with. And I might have made a couple mistakes.

In the summer of 1985, Reagan had a tumour removed from his colon. The public story was that he recovered quickly, but the truth was different. For months, all he could handle was the occasional speech, a state dinner here and there. Most of his time was spent in his suite. He read the briefings in bed with a cup of tea, Nancy worrying about his pillows. And I lounged in the Oval Office, a picture of recovery.

The first of December, I met with his advisers about the missiles we were shipping to the Middle East. We had the Israelis acting as middlemen between us and an Iranian opposition group; the Israelis gave the Iranians weapons, they handed us the money.

But during that meeting, Colonel North suggested a change of game plan. "If Israel gives the missiles to the Iranian army, Hezbollah will release their hostages."

"I won't negotiate with terrorists." It was a point Reagan was firm on.

"My contacts are moderates, against terrorism, Mr. President," said Colonel North.

I waited for someone else to argue the point. Money to the Iranian army? Hostages for weapons? But no one said a word. They were all watching me.

"Whatever you fellows feel is best," I said. My standard response under pressure.

A day later, when I ran into North again, he was on to Nicaragua.

I shook my head and veered for a getaway. "Violence is Nicaragua's main export." One of Reagan's favourite lines.

"What if we could fund the Contras without Congress getting involved?" North said. "We'd cut out Israel from the Iran deal. Sell the missiles direct, for a markup. Funnel the profits to the Contras."

"Two birds with a stone," I said. It didn't mean yes. I was musing—an important part of the act. But maybe North didn't see it as such.

Mostly I told Reagan everything I had agreed to, so that he could go back and renege on the promises I had made in his name. But sometimes, when I forgot the particulars, I didn't bother; I'd assume that if it was something important, it would be brought up again. Did North ever ask Reagan directly about the Contra deal? Maybe not. Some say Reagan was likely already suffering from Alzheimer's during the mess. He admitted to a guns-for-hostages swap, but swore he didn't know a thing about any money funnelled to the Nicaraguans. Maybe he didn't. And maybe I had a role in his undoing. Certainly, you won't argue with the fact that Reagan came undone.

After Reagan's second term, he and Nancy moved back to Bel Air. I stayed close to them; they still needed me. For speeches, charity fundraisers, dinners. Reagan was deteriorating, and he wasn't up for much.

He was only three years my senior, but every day he looked older. I started needing makeup to achieve authenticity. Enough that sometimes Nancy wondered aloud if it was worth it, if it wasn't time for Reagan to bow out of the spotlight. But Reagan had bowed out already; I knew Nancy meant me. Still, I didn't think the course she'd choose would be so final: a public farewell, Reagan announcing his journey to the sunset of his life.

My last visit to Bel Air was the day after the Alzheimer's letter was read to the world. Reagan finally put down the *TV Guide* when Nance brought us coffee and pink wafer cookies. I had seen her dress before, rose-coloured, hanging loose where once the fabric seemed to stretch over her hips. When she leaned against the door frame, I read exhaustion in the curve of her back. Her hem was torn. The fan on the side table moved over the hairs on my arm like wind across the lawn, and I kept my gaze fixed there, away from the frayed thread pressing itself to her calf.

"This isn't the way people will remember him," Nance said before she left the room. She did not believe Reagan would get better; she was stating the obvious. No one kept company with Reagan without an invitation from her, and now there wouldn't be any to be had.

The applause had died and the audience was dispersing. It was time for my curtain call. When Nance stepped into the hallway, I followed her. Yes, Reagan was in the next room, but what is a wife to a man with no memories? How long would it be until she too was a stranger to him? As he lost more and more of himself, she would be his comfort. Wasn't it fair, then, for her to take some comfort for herself? And so I did what I had seen him do so many times before.

But when I placed my hands on Nancy's shoulders, my

lips against her neck, her body turned rigid. She did not need to ask me to leave.

I forgive Nancy for what she did. The Secret Service men in my living room the day after my Bel Air visit, those once-friendly faces turned stiff and cold. I was to vacate my house, the country. I had forty-eight hours, and only one decision that was mine: I could fly or take the Toyota. The car I had named Sparrow; she was the same colour as Nancy's eyes. And so I drove.

These men I had known for years acted like they'd never met me. They acted like they hadn't ever taken a beer from my fridge, lost a pocketful of coins to me in a card game. When it's so easy for a fellow to change his tune about you, you start to wonder what your friendship with him meant to begin with. But they were doing their jobs.

The one thing I wish: that they hadn't watched me pack. I wanted to take something to remember her by. I had photographs, "to do" lists she had written, even a half-used tube of lipstick that fell from her purse once onto the floor of the car we were sharing.

They drove with me in a convoy all the way to the border; at night, my motel room was in lockdown mode. I could hear them through the wall, laughing, but I was Mr. Driscoll now. Not Double Dutch, like they had nick-named me. Not even Noah.

That first night, I had a nightmare: Colonel Ito

surrendering at the camp in Manchuria, passing his sword to an American officer. The sky over the compound white with parachutes dropping supplies and a Japanese guard dumping two-year-old Red Cross packages into my lap. You might think this would be a pleasant dream, but I'll tell you why it isn't. It is a dream about hope, about new beginnings. One should never convince oneself such things are possible.

At the Peace Arch, before they left me to myself, the Secret Service men delivered my sentence: "You will not be allowed re-entry into the United States. You will not be able to contact Mrs. Reagan. She thanks you for your service to the country and wishes to express her husband's gratitude."

Once the ferry docked in Victoria, I began the drive up-island. I pulled off the Malahat at Goldstream Park only to use the bathroom, but the crowd of children at the fence and the smell of decay led me to the river. The salmon were spawning: ragged carcasses lined the bank, fins torn to lace, and in the shallow water raw red fish thrashed upstream, returning to this place just in time to die. An eagle perched on a log, jabbing his beak into the split-open belly of a large salmon. I sat on a bench at the river's edge until long after the sun went down. I was eighty years old; I had nothing to show for my life.

I slept in the car, the Toyota alone in the lot but for a rusted bicycle that was chained to the fence—stripped of everything except its frame and one bent wheel. In my sleep, the Japs were marching us from Bataan, POWs to the left, Filipinos to the right. The same as it was, but the bodies heaped on the side of the road were salmon, our captors bending to slice open bellies with the knives they held in their fists. They scooped the pink roe with their blades, then raised it to their mouths as flies swarmed their lips and fingers. The soldier with my Timex on his wrist pointed at a woman in front of me. I watched her thin legs stumble over clothes and equipment those ahead of us had dropped, and knew suddenly and certainly that this was Nancy. I screamed a warning: *Run!* But she only turned to me with a blank stare.

And now I am parked in front of a row of apartment buildings where my brother's home once stood. Instead of my trailer, a parking lot; instead of the chicken coop, a row of saplings. The traces of my old life erased just as completely as the life I was removed from. While Ronald Reagan slips into oblivion with Nancy at his side, I am as alone as I always was. As I will always be. This is my final punishment—what a man gets for loving another man's wife.

⚜ ELECTROCUTING THE ELEPHANT

FREDERIC THOMPSON

The sandy ground was crisp with frost. His head pounded. He took a long pull from his flask, then tucked it in his pocket and drew his wool coat tight. Rather than watch the gathering crowd, he closed his eyes and imagined himself on a steamer chair in Luna's cabin, the only passenger aboard the cigar-shaped airship. He conjured the gong's crash and the whoosh of air as the pulleys flapped the colossal canvas wings. The deck was balanced on gimballed bearings, and soon it was undulating beneath his feet. The air roared louder as the ship strained against its cables. But this ride on Trip to the Moon was in reverse. The painted canvas behind the portholes scrolled backwards: the lunar volcano, the canyons and craters, the sunlit clouds, starlight, darkness. Then the storm: lightning flashes, the roll of thunder, heavy bursts of rain on the awning. When the storm ebbed, Earth appeared in the distance—a speck, then a globe, then a wash of blue and green that filled the glass. Soon the blinking lights of the city were visible as the ship zoomed towards the exhibition grounds and finally landed.

He could hear the hum of the crowd over the wind, but he kept his eyes squeezed shut. He pictured himself debarking the airship, then imagined a stroll through the Luna Park that existed only in his imagination, in the plans that papered his desk: Past the double Ferris wheel he'd dubbed the Aerio Cycle—its opposing wheels see-sawing as they spun. Past the submarine trip to the North Pole, where visitors floated beside octopuses, seals, and mermaids, then disembarked to tour an Eskimo village. Past dance halls and swimming pools, aerial acts, circus rings, ticket sellers in evening gowns perched atop Roman chariots, a miniature railroad, an authentic Dutch wind-mill, a village of uncivilized tribesmen. Past Venice in New York, with its colonnades and its Grand Canal full of gondolas. Past re-created battles between miniature navies in the War of the Worlds building. Past brass bands on platforms, boatloads of passengers squealing down Shoot-the-Chutes, elephants and camels strolling the grounds with children perched on their backs. Past spire after spire, minaret after minaret, all of them glowing. And at the centre of it all, beside the lagoon, the Electric Tower—two hundred feet high and studded with half a million bulbs of electric wonder. A billion-dollar smile for Coney Island.

He opened his eyes. The grounds of Luna Park were

a maze of scaffolding, barren stretches of concrete, mounds of dirt. The airship was beached near the fence. It was more ornithopter than dirigible, but stripped of its wings it resembled only an enormous canoe. The building that was to house it was nothing more than stacks of lumber. Even the Electric Tower was unfinished. He'd had to pull the carpenters off it last week — redirect them to the lagoon in front of Shoot-the-Chutes. Instead of constructing Luna Park's siren song, they had fashioned a platform for an execution and a bridge sturdy enough to hold the weight of the condemned: Topsy, the elephant.

At least Shoot-the-Chutes was complete, a relic left over from Sea Lion Park. His men had positioned the photographers directly across from it, on the east side of the lagoon. Well in view of the banners declaring Luna Park's Grand Opening, May 1903.

He pulled out his flask. He had promised Dundy he'd press Bets-a-Million Gates and George Kessler for a commitment, but this could wait. They were both on the risers now, the latter with his wife and kids, as if this was just another Sunday picnic on Coney Island.

Maybe they should have held off until spring, when the park opened. At least the crowds could have been let inside, rather than turned away as per orders of the ASPCA. There were a number of spectators, but only newspapermen, the Edison team, the Coney Island

Elite—none of whom had parted with so much as a penny for the privilege. Aside from a handful of young boys who'd slipped through the fence, the common folk had drifted away, though some only as far as the tavern across Surf Avenue. They were on the roof, their admission quarters clearly spent on drink. The air was damp and cold, not a day for an outing to Coney Island—especially with the electricity out.

May might have been better, but they couldn't have waited. They couldn't have kept Topsy alive that long. They were already stretched from the costs of construction, and she ate twenty-five dollars of hay a week. Not to mention the expense of a real elephant man. Just hiring Carl Goliath for the day had cost as much as they'd paid Whitey per week. And though the expense associated with her keep had seemed tolerable when he'd counted on children clamouring for rides, the newspapers were calling Topsy a man killer. There wasn't a mother in New York who'd perch her darlings on the beast's back.

When noon struck, there was a murmur through the crowd and Thompson turned to see the elephant approaching. Dundy was on her right and Goliath on her left, with a rake in his hand, prodding the monster behind her ear. Two of the bigger Italians on the construction crew trailed behind. The elephant wore a martingale harness, her trunk wrapped with chains affixed to the leather belt around her middle. Still, four men would be no match for the beast if she decided to liberate herself in the eleventh hour.

They continued through the construction site and past the long line of spectators on the risers, towards the lagoon and the bridge that led out to the platform—a narrow reinforced plank. Then, no more than twenty feet from it, she stopped.

The crowd was silent as Topsy stood frozen in place. George Kessler took out his pocket watch and tilted it towards his wife. She had her coat unbuttoned, their youngest child wrapped inside it. She whispered something in her husband's ear. The men on the tavern roof grew restless. Though he couldn't make out their words, he knew they were taunting—either him or the elephant, it made no difference. Laughter followed. He darted a glance at Murray, the press agent, who had joined Dundy at the elephant's side. It was Murray who'd assured him and Dundy that the event would be a money-maker, that things would go off without a hitch. And it was him that Thompson intended to axe if this did not come to pass. Murray returned his glance, then reached for the bag of carrots at his feet. He dropped one near the bridge and Topsy shuffled forwards and reached for it with her trunk. She curled it into her mouth, then arced her trunk towards him for more. Murray complied, but the rest of the carrots the elephant only stretched for. Thompson counted them. Twenty-seven carrots in her mouth and not another step.

He caught Dundy's eye and his partner shrugged.

Goliath was leaned towards Topsy, muttering in her ear, but she kept her lazy eyes averted. Then Goliath swung her round and returned up the path towards the animal quarters, and the crowd on the tavern roof began to boo. Goliath and Topsy made it to the edge of Shoot-the-Chutes then turned again, a repeat approach, but the elephant stopped at the same place. Thompson drew his coat tighter. It would be impossible to convince Gates and Kessler that his plans for Luna Park would ever material-ize if he couldn't even dispose of a stubborn pachyderm.

Thompson pushed through the crowd to a huddle of men at the fence — some of the construction crew. He picked out a blond one rubbing his arms through his sleeves. No sense wasting time on an Italian.

"You know where Whitey is?" he asked.

The man shook his head. "I could find him, though, sir."

"You offer him twenty-five dollars to get the beast on the scaffold. Now."

Thompson had been skeptical of this from the begin-ning — aware of the possible catastrophes, primarily that the event might cost more than it brought in, when there was barely any money left to lose. It was a fact that elephant executions didn't draw crowds anymore. Barnum and Bailey killed five during their last European tour. A sixth aboard the ship once they'd docked in New York. That one they strangled with a rope hitched to a steam-powered winch — a donkey engine — then they weighted it down with three tons of pig iron and dumped it off a seagoing tug. But Murray said if things were done right, people would come.

Electricity, he'd declared. It was a risk: the electrocution of an elephant had been attempted only once. Thompson had been at the Pan-American Exposition then, and well recalled. It hadn't worked. But this was because Edison hadn't been involved, Murray claimed. And couldn't Thompson remember the crowd — salivating? Yes, it was true. He did remember that.

And the crowd had come, hadn't they? About that, Murray had been right. He had sent the advance men to poster New York, had the power plant ensure the trolley cars were running when the rest of the electricity on Coney Island had been switched off to build a charge for the beast. But then the ASPCA arrived. First to say they couldn't use electricity — only relenting when Thompson himself assured them it was the best method. That they did not intend to copy the Central Park Zoo, their executed elephant, Tip, requiring two doses of poisoned bran, and only keeling over fifty-four convulsions later. Electrocution was quick, and painless. Had not the New York state legislature adopted the electric chair the year before? Also, the wizard himself would be involved. And they would poison the elephant first, then strangle her with a donkey engine as soon as the current was switched off, ensuring she was thoroughly dead.

The ASPCA had capitulated, but not about the

audience. Apparently it was unethical, illegal even, to invite paying spectators to an animal's execution. They'd had to turn back the throng outside the gate, and the quarter per viewer Murray had promised—enough to more than make up for the expenses involved—hadn't materialized.

At least he'd thought to erect banners behind the beast advertising the park's opening. He'd had the men hang one facing every direction, the letters a foot high. With Edison's men filming the event, every audience member in every nickelodeon in the country would soon know about Luna Park. Which would be a further embarrassment if a botched execution drained his funds and scared off investors. If Luna never materialized.

At least Topsy was worth something dead. The taxidermist was by the fence with his kit. He'd skin the elephant as soon as she was pronounced dead, assuming she could be coaxed onto the scaffold. They'd donate the heart and stomach to Princeton's biology department, but the hide was worth fourteen dollars a square foot, and there were paying takers for the bones and even the intestines. He and Dundy would keep the legs for umbrella stands: one for each of them, the other two to garner favours.

Kessler stepped off the risers, motioning his wife and children ahead of him. Thompson should have stopped them. Bought the boys a bag of nuts, draped his coat around the wife's shoulders, pulled Kessler himself aside and shared with him his vision of the inevitable majesty of Luna Park. He should have, but instead he averted his eyes as they passed. Then he pulled out his flask and took another drink.

TOPSY

They led her from the stable. At her flank, the one who turned herd leader when the true two-foot leader wasn't present. At her ear, an echo of two-feet past—in costume, in words, in the poke of metal into her skin. Behind these two were two others—herd outsiders. Ones who'd once scrambled up the tower when she dropped her load and charged towards it.

She had charged many times. Sometimes Whitey had whistled her down before she reached the wooden structure. Sometimes he'd let her slam her forelegs on the boards, stretch her trunk towards the two-feet's ankles. Listen to them trumpet. She did not cause pain, only fear. For Whitey.

Soon the tower would be lit, that's what Whitey said. The lights so bright it would never be night on Coney Island. She could imagine it: glowing like star-dazzle beneath sky cloth. But today the tower was empty, and dark. The air was cold. Wind blew sand against her flank.

The two-feet led her towards a gathering of their kind. There were males mostly. She saw the true-herd leader among them. He lifted his eyes to her, then pulled them away. There was warming-water in his hand, always there was warming-water in his hand, but he didn't share. Only Whitey did. She searched for Whitey among the faces. Whitey, who stroked care into her flank with his hands. Who had hurt her, but whom she forgave. He wasn't there.

In a drift of sand was the ship built for air. She closed her eyes and remembered the day Whitey roped her to it. When she'd stepped forwards, the thick ropes had sliced valleys into her skin. When she'd stepped again, the valleys became blood-rivers. She had dipped her head, found Whitey's eyes with her own. He hadn't untied her, only disappeared into the herd of two-feet.

She'd heard the two-feet's calls—a strange trumpeting. Then she shuffled backwards until the ropes became slack. Whitey returned, his voice sharp in her ears, and next his three-prong in her flesh—sharper still.

She'd been anchored. She could not have done what Whitey asked, but even then she knew this two-foot was hers. She could not hurt him. Would not. And still he had prodded her. She felt it all again. Slamming: lumber against sand. Shrieking: a two-foot female. Heaving: her own breath. Then the pain had ended. Whitey untied the rope. He loosened her harness. His rough palm cared her side.

He had let her go, and so she did go, down the wide path with two-feet in her wake. But not Whitey. When she turned to find him, he was being dragged the opposite direction, slumped between a pair of blue-coated two-feet, clubs swinging in their hands. But still she had carried on. She had carried on until the two-feet behind her grew to a swarm, a mob. There were ropes thrown—one, two, three around her neck. She had let herself be led back into the stable then. She hoped Whitey would be there. But he wasn't, not until later. He came in small, with the two-feet herd leader beside him.

She should not have left him, and the next time she did not. She followed him and the blue-coats. And that had been worse.

Now Whitey was gone again, but the blue-coats were there among the two-feet herd. She was led past them by a metal poke behind her ear. With pokes she was guided alongside a ribbon of wire. Whitey had learned to guide her with his palms. With his words.

Who were these other two-feet? This horde of two-feet? Were they here to watch her? She could do so many tricks: walk a wire, play a horn, dance. Were they here to trumpet for her? Thunder their feet? Feed her sweets from their palms? But she had no herd to accompany her.

She looked again at the wire on the ground. It led across a bridge over the lagoon, then ended on an island of lumber. This is where she was to perform, then. They would attach her to the wire and she would become the star dazzle. She would tear open the sky with her light. She would be amazing.

But where were all the small two-feet? There was only

a scattering of them among the full-size males. Also, it was too cold. It was too quiet. No, she would not perform for these two-feet. Only for Whitey. She knew what two-feet were capable of. She stood still and the metal poked again behind her ear. But she would not move. She did not trust these others.

She closed her eyes and saw herself before she'd been bound to stillness. The leather strap around her head, the chains that held her trunk, all this was gone. Early sun glowed through the sky-cloth as she stood among her herd-not-herd. There were males on both sides, unlike in child-hood: her mother, and the others—mothers and mothers and mothers. Of course, their leader, the mother of them all—blind, older than earth. This non-herd had no leader, or maybe it was led by two-feet. There was one of them in front of her—with a glass in his hand, with a mouth-fire in his lips. She knew him from among the trumpeting two-feet at the bright-nights. At the bright-nights city after city after city. She could smell warming-water, but his loose wrist proved his glass was empty. He tilted it towards her, but she did not move her trunk. He thrust it closer. His call filled her ears. She was tired still and closed her eyes. Through her feet she sensed a shuffle in the sand, and then a gust of grit hit her face. She opened her eyes to the two-foot dusting clean his hands. The glass was on the ground, but the mouth-fire was between his fingers. He shoved it against the tip of her trunk. The pain of it. The pain. Pain.

And what she did next—what she did as her herd-not-herd trumpeted on all sides of her: wrapped her trunk around the two-foot, lifted him, cracked him open against the earth. The sound his body made she could both hear and feel — through her feet and into her blood. And then her foot up and over and down before she could stop herself. He was still finally. And she knew, dead. She rocked back and forth, she swung her trunk, she bobbed her head, she shook her feet — trying to slip off the guilt that closed in on her. But even then there was a part of her body that guilt didn't cover. A part of her that felt glad, glad she had ended the suffering of it. And it was that part that made her do it again, and again, and again. Three more two-feet cracked against the ground. The fear in their eyes — that they should feel what she felt. But the others she let live.

These men with her now she could hurt also, but she wouldn't. She didn't want to. Maybe if she waited, Whitey would be returned to her. So she would wait.

Another two-foot came with carrots. He held one out and she wrapped her trunk around it, then swung it to her mouth. He placed another on the cold sand and she shuffled forwards, then he placed another past it. Carrot after carrot leading her towards the lagoon. She would not fall for this. And he had not considered her trunk. She stretched it out to reach for the farthest carrot first. When the two-foot knelt down to move one farther, she swung her head towards him, her trunk outstretched, and he backed away.

The two-feet knew she would not go to the lagoon.
The one with the metal turned her around, led her back
towards the stables. She had defeated them. A loud trumpeting came from the sky. She looked up and there was a
pack of two-feet perched on top of a building. Was Whitey
with them?

No.

And then she was swung back around. She was led
back towards the lagoon. But she stopped in the same
place. The metal poked behind her ear. A huddle of two-
feet left the herd; they walked away. Let them all leave.
She would not perform for them. She would not move.
She would not.

WILLIAM "WHITEY" ALT

Twenty-five dollars wasn't enough to lead Topsy to her
death. Even a thousand dollars wasn't enough. He may
have been a drunk and a louse, a welcher, but he was no
murderer.

He'd hoped to sleep through the execution, but once
he'd been shaken out of his stupor he figured he'd hide
himself in the back of the crowd. He owed it to Topsy to
attend her funeral, if it could be called that.

He couldn't shake the guilt. Every time he closed his
eyes, it was like he was in a nickelodeon, watching a replay
of the first time things turned ugly at Luna. There'd been
a squall: gusts blasting sand against his face until his skin

was raw and his eyes burned. The whole morning, he had led the elephant up and down Surf Avenue, Topsy dragging the exterior beams of the airship building from Steeplechase Park, lining the beams into two rows like rail tracks. Every time she placed them wrong, he'd have to reposition them himself, his back strained, his fingers aching, as the elephant stood over him and rocked her trunk, her chains rattling, her rank, heavy breath against his neck.

He'd spent the night before on the Bowery, and all he'd wanted was sleep. Either that or another drink to smooth himself out. The work was slow, the wind sharp, the Italians loud, and he was fed up with all of it.

Once the workers had dismantled the building, they'd slathered the beams with grease. The plan was for Topsy to drag the airship along the makeshift track all the way to Luna Park. Then she'd be sent to retrieve the greased beams, Whitey following after her while the Italians smoked cigarettes and watched. But when Whitey had tied her to the airship, she'd taken a single step then lurched to a stop.

Was it possible she couldn't pull it? Maybe. But without wings, the airship was nothing more than an aluminum hull. It was huge, but then so was the elephant. More likely she just *wouldn't*.

He'd asked the foreman for a glass of whisky — for the elephant. She had a taste for drink, and they all knew it. But Hugh Thomas, he'd said no. All of them standing there, the Italians yipping nonsense and Hugh Thomas muttering that Whitey was *some elephant man*. He'd lost it. He'd grabbed the pitchfork and jabbed at Topsy's sides. He hadn't meant to hurt her. Her sagging hide was thick as big-top canvas. In truth, he hadn't registered the blood right away. Once he did, he felt remorseful. Sure he did. When he took off her harness and let her wander down the strip, it was an apology of sorts. He was giving her a break from it. Nobody saw it as such, but that's what it was. And then he was arrested and Topsy was lassoed and dragged back to Luna Park by the cops. The *Brooklyn Eagle* published it all front page: TOPS, THE BAD ELEPHANT, MAKES TROUBLE AT CONEY. Or at least that's what Thompson claimed when he read Whitey the riot act.

To slip inside Luna for the execution, he bribed the Italian at that gate with everything in his pockets, which wasn't much. When he got to the edge of the crowd, he saw her, wearing the martingale harness, and chained by all four feet to construction pilings at the edge of the lagoon. Over the lagoon was a platform. A noose fashioned from thick rope lay on top. Beside it, a smokestack rising from a mess of cranks and levers — a donkey engine. A few men pulled down a beam and lugged it across the bridge. The electricians were extending the wires Whitey had followed the length of Surf Avenue, wires that ended where Topsy had been meant to place her feet. He turned away and retched against the fence.

She had killed men: three, he'd heard. This was before Whitey's time. Two trainers, and a tourist who'd fed her a cigarette, the fink. And yet the last straw for Thompson had been something so harmless in comparison. A mistake.

Whitey had changed after that day with the airship. Topsy had offered him something that he hadn't had a chance at before. Was it too much to call it redemption? Like all the females he'd ever known, she had a long memory. But unlike the rest, she didn't hold a grudge. The blood, the pitchfork, she had forgiven all of it. He tried harder for her. It was possible, he realized, to be different.

It happened a month after the incident with the airship. A wagon of lumber was stuck in a pothole and the foreman wanted Topsy to push it out with her forehead. She refused, and Whitey'd poked her. Not hard, but as soon as he did it, he knew it was wrong. She turned with those deep eyes, those long lashes, and just stared at him. So he climbed onto her neck and together they set off down Surf Avenue. He'd needed a drink, and intended to buy her one also.

She felt affection for him. Why else would she have followed him to the police station after he was arrested? Followed him up the front steps, then through the door until she was wedged half in, half out. The noise she'd made. He could have quieted her if they'd let him. Instead, they'd all scattered and he was left alone in the backroom cuffed to a chair. Thompson came for the elephant but bailed Whitey out as well when she wouldn't move for anyone else. The next day, Topsy was off the crew, and half a dozen Italians were sent to the station to fix the splintered wood around the doorway. That one made the *New York Times*: ELEPHANT TERRORIZES CONEY ISLAND POLICE. *You understand we rely on the goodwill of the police?* Thompson had said when he shoved the paper towards him. *Any ideas on how to get that back?* Whitey had just shaken his head. He knew his time at Luna Park was over, but he hadn't considered Thompson would dispose of him and the elephant both.

The beam was erected beside Topsy. The noose was looped around her neck, then hooked to the steam donkey. The electricians moved two wooden footpads from the scaffold onto the sandy earth. Then that bastard Murray fed her carrots. *Hollowed out*, came the whispers through the crowd. *Filled with cyanide.* So unsuspecting. She took them straight from his palm.

He wanted to go to her, plead for forgiveness. But Thompson had made it clear Whitey wasn't ever to set foot in Luna. Not to mention that Captain Knipe was only feet from him, along with the police reserves. He was ashamed of himself, abandoning her there. He was ashamed. He was ashamed. Only thing in his life he'd ever felt proud of was being an elephant man.

TOPSY

Whitey had come. She saw him now behind the other two-feet. His herd leader had allowed his return in time for her performance, for the shine of her body. And for Whitey, she would perform. If he led her to the lagoon, she would follow him. If he stood on the island of lumber, she would stand beside him.

She saw herself as she had been at so many bright-nights beneath the sky-cloth, when the star-dazzle that opened the dark had come from above her head and not from beneath her skin. Then, her herd-not-herd had surrounded her. They stood in the shadows and watched two-feet swing near the sky-cloth, walk wires in the air. And then it had been their turn.

The two-feet rose to standing at the edges of the sky-cloth. They trumpeted; they thundered their feet. In front of them, Topsy spun, she pounded music-makers with her trunk, with the pads of her feet. She knelt, then rolled to rest on her head. Surrounding her, her herd-not-herd did the same.

She had no herd-not-herd with her now, but she could still do these things. She would do these things for Whitey with her new glowing body. But Whitey was curled small. He was turned away.

There would be pain, then. Whitey knew it. She had felt pain before the bright-nights of her past. Ropes fastened to her forelegs and trunk, leather belts tightened around her middle, the two-feet had pulled her into position again, and again, and again. Topsy learned fast. The dark two-foot had held peanuts to her trunk and stroked care into her side. The pale two-foot had a wooden pole with a spike on the end. When she stumbled, he thrust it into her flank, thrust it over and over and over until she cried, until she wailed, until she hallooed. And then he'd trumpeted his victory. And she had been broken. Every time she had been broken, not just the time he did break her—her tail bent crooked forever after.

There were two-feet on the lumber island now, more herd outsiders. They tore the island apart while others dragged the wood down the bridge and slammed it onto the sand beside her. Still more came to pound metal stakes near her feet. The two-feet beside her had rope. They tied it to the metal, then to her legs.

She had spent so much time tied still. But not in the beginning. Not when she was with her first herd-not-herd: just five adults, males and females both, and her only a child. So young she should have been with her mother, should have drunk from her mother and not eaten hay. But her mother had been gone then: dead, lost, Topsy didn't know. At night, stars had lit the wide-open sky and the air was cold, always cold. And she had walked behind the others along the hard path called tracks. Night after night she had done this, from town to town to town. This had been misery, but soon it had become a misery she longed for. When she was crammed with the others in a metal box to be jolted, jarred, jangled as they raced along the tracks, two-feet asleep above their heads. And the only walking was from the boxes to underneath the sky-cloth and back again, so that even when she was chained, she had to shuffle her feet to feel the movement that her body wanted to make, needed to make, but could not.

She shuffled her feet now and the two-feet jumped away from her. All but a pack of herd outsiders, who continued to build a tower of wood at her side. Whitey had never tied her down. With Whitey she had walked: up and down the sandy path beside the ocean. Whitey walked beside her, or sometimes he sat on her back. He was not heavy; she did not mind. And if Whitey told her to stop, she would stop. But these two-feet did not trust her.

She felt a rope slip over her head and turned to see the two-foot with the metal poker. He had the rope end in his hand. Her head fastened also? He passed the rope to the two-foot outsiders and they carried it to the top of the tower of wood, then threw it over.

When the two-feet had taught her to dance, they had tied her neck like this. Then they had pulled her to standing on her hind legs. But she could not dance with these ropes on her legs. She shuffled her feet again.

The two-foot with carrots came with more. Larger ones. Bitter ones. He held them on his palm for her to eat. In the sky-cloth days, there had been peanuts, popcorn, sweets. She would eat them from the sticky palms of small two-feet. Afterwards, they would stroke her trunk with their tiny hands. They would stare into her eyes.

But this two-foot didn't look at her. And his carrots were foul-tasting. She would not have eaten them, except that she was hungry. All she had been given for days was hay, damp hay, rotting hay, hay briny from the ocean air.

The two-feet herd was shifting. There was a low-rumble of sound. Anticipation. She knew this from the sky-cloth days. It was almost time for her performance. But she had no idea what they intended her to do.

THOMAS ALVA EDISON

Thompson had asked him to flip the switch, and he'd refused. Thompson was a showman, and Edison could imagine the posters: *The Wizard of Electricity to Personally Execute the Condemned!* Another draw for the paying spectators — none of whom had been allowed inside the gates.

Though Edison had little respect for Thompson's profession, he did respect the quality of his efforts. Edison had attended the Pan-American Exposition on Midway Day, the day Thompson had convinced the organizers to turn the fair over to him. Edison was not interested in base entertainment — a daredevil sliding down a rope by his teeth, the release of ten thousand carrier pigeons, a race between a camel, an ostrich, an elephant, and a man. Yet he had been impressed by Thompson's ability to draw a crowd, and impressed further by the man's "airship" — which was a mechanically sound structure, albeit one that could not actually lift off the ground.

Edison no longer cared about the things that had for so long occupied his mind: deadly current — alternating versus direct. And he did not enjoy Coney Island even in temperate weather. His respect for Thompson played a large part in his willingness to dispatch the elephant. His respect, and a small surge of curiosity — all traces of which had faded long before he got to this construction site cum execution chamber.

He had arrived with the Kinetograph and its large wooden tripod, along with the young men he'd trained to operate the machine. He had stood by as they'd set up at the edge of the lagoon and trained the lens on the empty platform. Then he'd offered his final directive: there was only so much celluloid film inside the machine. It was imperative they hold off until the moment the current was switched on, so as to guarantee the capture of the elephant's death.

And then he had stood at the edge of the stands and pulled his hat down, turned his deaf ear towards anyone who approached.

Some wizard he was. The only thing he had conjured in the second half of his life was his own misfortune. He had been erased completely from Edison Electric — his name, his stake. In fact, the few electric plants still loyal to his name were without exception unfaithful to his ideals. They used generating units designed by Westinghouse.

Then there was the Kinetoscope, a machine he had intended for educational purposes but which didn't generate a profit until he created moving images of boxing cats, wrestling dogs, trained bears, Princess Ali the belly dancer. Also the more lurid scenes: the Indian Scalping, the Lynching, the Execution of Mary, Queen of Scots. But these had only held attention for as long as people were content to gaze through a keyhole. Not long.

He'd had no hand in inventing "Edison's Vitascope" — the larger-than-life screen used in the nickelodeons — only a desperation for funds that spurred him to sell his name. Those funds he had poured into his iron ore project — a method to excavate depleted mines. Poured it as one pours water down a drain. As soon as every last cent was gone, high-grade ore was discovered in Minnesota so close to the surface that a single man with a steam shovel could scoop up fifty tons in three minutes.

The Vitascope was all that he had left, its origins nothing to be proud of. Let alone the first pictures it played — two dancers, a wave breaking on a beach. Worst of all, May Irwin's fifteen-second kiss.

The portable taking machine, the Kinetograph, was his at least. He had made moving pictures of Niagara Falls, of elephant tricks, but not of McKinley's assassination, though he was at the Pan-American at the time. The machine was set up at the exit, ready to film the president as he left. There were no images of Leon Czolgosz, nor of the man who punched the gun from his hands. Instead, just a blurred shot of people running from the exit. The film he'd titled: *Outside the Temple of Music After the President Was Shot*. Another failure.

He'd had a chance to save McKinley. He sent an X-ray machine to find the bullet the surgeons couldn't locate. The machine was capable of spotting a nickel placed under the back of a man of considerable girth. The doctors didn't use it. They thought the president would heal naturally. Instead, he'd died of gangrene. Hence the next picture: *Funeral Cortege Entering Westlawn Cemetery*. The following one came after he was denied permission to take a moving picture of Czolgosz's execution. It was partly authentic, partly staged: *Execution of Czolgosz with Panorama of Auburn Prison*. Topsy's execution would be the first real death he'd captured. This was no victory. He did not feel fulfillment, standing in the cold near a docile beast who'd been sentenced to death.

And the elephant *was* docile, though the press referred to her as a man killer. The elephant man stood behind her and tapped a rear foot with his cane, and she knelt on the dirt and lifted it towards him. He strapped the plate on and she stood again. Then the man went round to her front and tapped her right foot and she lifted it. He slipped the electrode underneath and cinched the strap, but when she stepped down, the crack was audible — the wood splintering under her weight. He tapped again and she lifted again, but the electrode must have been intact because he let her set her foot down.

Edison had designed these death sandals. They were twelve-inch copper electrodes affixed to wooden boards cut to the shape of the elephant's feet. He selected the feet because of their fleshy pads, removed from major bones—settled on the front right and hind left to create a cross-current. The copper wire affixed to the electrodes travelled nine blocks, to Coney's electric plant. The straps were so that Topsy could not escape the current once it was switched on, though he suspected her weight alone would ensure the necessary contact. The current he had only guessed at: 6600 volts. More than ten times the amount that had killed a horse, but then the beast was at least ten times the size the old mare had been.

There was a time when he'd been desperate for a hand in the electrocution of an elephant. In designing New York State's electric chair, he had executed forty-four dogs, two calves, the mare, of course, which he'd paid eleven dollars for—ten for the animal, the eleventh to have her led to his lab. He'd wrapped the electrodes in cloth soaked in salt water, then tied them to her legs. She didn't die until he increased the voltage to 600 for twenty-five seconds. The resulting mess took half a day to clean.

He had been promised Forepaugh's elephant, Chief, who was rumoured to have murdered eleven men. Forepaugh had contacted Edison when the elephant broke free from his quarters and charged at his trainer and a group of local women. The old man had armed ten marksmen with the breech-loading rifles used in re-enactments of Custer's Last Stand. The bullets had only enraged the beast, caused him to break free from his chains, to trumpet, to bellow, this noise causing a chain reaction among the lions, the tigers, and the monkey house. Finally, when the blood was streaming, the elephant went down, and the call was made for Edison to proceed to the show's winter quarters to dispatch of the beast more completely. But Forepaugh's son had taken matters into his own hands before Edison arrived. He killed the elephant by death line: a rope around its neck affixed to two chains, and those chains affixed to two other elephants prodded in opposite directions. There had been other promises after this one, but never one that materialized.

He had wanted to execute an elephant when that execution would have proved a point: the danger of alternating current over direct current. The danger of being—as he had assumed it would be known—"Westinghoused." But of course that was already over. Every man condemned to death in New York was electrocuted by alternating current, yet this detail had proved irrelevant. In the war of the currents, alternating had been declared the winner. The safer, better option never prevailed over the cheaper one.

Dundy, Thompson's partner, secured the final rope to the harness around Topsy's head, and then he and the other men backed away from the animal. Dundy was not a brilliant man, only a well-heeled one, and Edison respected him much less than he respected Thompson. In fact, he respected him not at all.

The elephant stood still and silent. There was not a
ripple of sound in the crowd. Even the wind had quieted.
Because of his Kinetograph, after her death Topsy would
continue to live on in every nickelodeon in the country.
That was one way to consider it. He supposed the other
way was more sinister: because of him, Topsy's death
would be endlessly repeated.

TOPSY

She felt strange. Her blood moved slowly through her
body, her thoughts pushed upwards to hover near the
edge of her skin.

The two-foot with the metal tapped her rear foot,
and she knelt on the dirt and lifted it towards him. She
did not think to do this, but just watched it happen. Saw
herself submit. The two-foot strapped a piece of wood
on her foot and she stood. Then he circled her body
and tapped her front right foot. This foot she tried to
hold firm to the ground, but it lifted also. It lifted, and
he strapped on another piece of wood, and she stepped
down and the wood splintered. It poked into her skin.
And she lifted it again, for the two-foot to take it off, for
the two-foot to pull the shards of wood out of her flesh.
But he only shifted it and then stepped away. And she
put her foot down.

She was bound completely now. She could not even
shuffle her feet. It reminded her of something. Of what?

She closed her eyes and darkness fell as the memory slipped over her. She could see nothing. She could only smell the foul dankness, feel the icy air and the rising and falling, rising and falling of waves beneath her. Her rear legs were chained in place and her trunk was wrapped around a pole. Her body rocked and swayed, her stomach lurched, and her feet shuffled to keep their balance. The hay at her feet was rotten and damp, but even still, when the ocean was smooth, she unwrapped her trunk to eat. Or she unwrapped her trunk to tuck it between her fore-legs, to warm it for a moment, to briefly escape the sharp and staggering cold. The only sounds were the clanging on the ship, the waves against the hull, and her own voice: her rumbling long-distance calls to her mother, to her other-mothers, to her true herd. Also her screams, shrill cries that kept on even while she slept.

She forced the memory off and opened her eyes. The ribbon of wire had split into two, and each was attached to her feet. She tried to find the other end, but it snaked into the distance as far as she could see. The two-feet around her had backed away. They were silent. All the two-feet were silent. Their herd leader clasped his warming-water in both hands. His eyes were closed. She was afraid; she needed Whitey to rescue her. Where was Whitey? She looked and found him halfway over the fence, scrambling away, making his retreat. Gone from her. Just like...

Just like...

No, she did not want this memory. She did not want it. But it charged towards her. It tackled her and held her down and she saw lushness, green. Her mother was there, her mother-mother. Topsy was tucked in the shade beneath her. The other mothers had formed a circle around them, to keep her safe. But she was not safe. There were two other elephants, elephants she did not know. And atop each sat a pair of two-feet, rope in their arms.

The two strange elephants separated the herd mother. They pushed into the circle on either side of her, squeezing her flanks. The two-feet slipped to the ground and tied their ropes around her legs, around her neck. And then they led the strange elephants away, the herd mother clamped between them, dragged along. Between the legs of the circle of mothers, Topsy saw other strange elephants. She saw other two-feet. More and more and more in every direction.

The other mothers were hauled off. Those who struggled were slammed with poles, were sliced with spears. Last of all, they came for Topsy's mother. Topsy stayed in her mother's shade. Stayed as her mother was led into the forest, as she was tied between tree trunks. It was then that the two-feet came for Topsy. They lassoed her neck and pulled, trees splintering as her mother struggled and hallooed. Topsy was tied to a pole, a pole that was carried through the forest—a pair of two-feet on each end—her scrabbling feet barely touching the ground. She cried for her mother, and her mother answered. She answered, and answered again, her voice growing softer. And then a time came when Topsy's cries were met with silence.

She pushed herself free of that memory, and she saw

the man with the black hat. The wizard, is that what the two-feet called him? But what did that mean? He had stepped away from the other two-feet, right to the edge of the lagoon. He had his hat under his arm now and his eyes on her. None of the two-feet had let her hold their eyes, but he did. He kept his eyes tight to hers and he bobbed his head and she wondered if he saw her fear. If he would untie her ropes. But he did not move. He bobbed his head and bobbed his head and then flame zinged her feet. Flame, and then an ocean-width of pain. Worse than Whitey's three-prong, or the pale two-foot's hook. Worse even than the mouth-fire touched to her trunk. Her blood screamed, then pushed against her skin until her body quaked and shuddered, out of her control. And she held his eyes and he nodded his head and he nodded his head. And then there was fire. She knew fire.

She closed her eyes and travelled backwards, to before her mother was taken from her. Again, Topsy was tucked into her shade, but this time they were both moving. Faster and faster they pounded through the forest, the other mothers in front and behind. Fire licked the green in three directions, and they ran the only way they could. The trees pressed tighter, but the mothers pushed for-wards. They trumpeted. They ripped up saplings with their trunks. They flattened branches with their feet. And then they reached a clearing.

But this was not safety. This clearing had walls — a lacing of wood. And along the length of them, wide, empty rivers dug into the earth. On the other side were two-feet—the first she had ever seen. Their hands held spears, and flames, and metal rods that cracked open the sky. The others surrounded Topsy and her mother, then turned to face the walls. They wheezed sharp breaths and rapped the ground with their trunks. The sound pushed through Topsy's feet and into her ears. She reached her trunk forwards, and her mother wrapped her own around it.

She opened her eyes, but she could not see the wizard now. All she could see was smoke. It billowed from her body and the pain billowed with it. It seemed impossible for it to grow, but it did grow. It swelled and spread until there was barely room for her in her body. Until she had been squeezed into a small kernel of herself, and that kernel was thrust upwards. It was thrust upwards until it was pressing against her skin. Harder and harder it pressed. And then it broke through and the pain was gone.

She hovered there over her smoke-blurred flesh-self, chained by the lagoon. Hovered over the island of lumber, the thick ribbons of cloth that flapped in the wind, the two-foot faces. And then she lifted away. She lifted until she was again beneath her mother, again encircled by her true herd. But this time her trunk hung limp as she drank with her mouth. There were no two-feet, no flames, only a green world. A blue swath of sky. Brown dust underfoot: so soft. But softer still, the trunks of her mothers, all of them touching her, stroking care into her at once.

She longed to stay in this perfect moment with her true herd. To be forever with her mother, her other mothers, all those gentle, sturdy bodies. But she lifted again. She lifted into a place of warmth, where she was both held close and floating, where light and sound were muffled until they ceased to exist. Until she felt her own existence slipping. Could this place be her eternity?

But then her senses jolted awake as her body was clenched tight and thrust down.

The ground shook as she hit the dirt. Her ears flapped open and caught sound: the trumpeting celebration of elephants. Or perhaps words — *turn off the current.*

Then darkness enfolded her completely.

HANDS LIKE BIRDS

The sun has set by the time the shuttle reaches Niagara Falls, and the main strip is shadows and throbbing neon. I shut my eyes because it's useless: I can't see the sidewalk anyways. All I can do is hug the side of the bus door and dig my foot through the air for solid ground. Finally, Dad clasps my shoulders and steers me to Jan—the Anne Sullivan to my Helen Keller. She grabs my fingers and squeezes before I yank away. The air is still and heavy. Hot. Then puffs of breeze as bodies pass, footsteps shuddering the sidewalk. I shuffle sideways, to feel Jan without having to touch her, when my foot catches. She doesn't reach out to steady me and my palms scuff the cement. Beside me are blue flashes, a streak of red, darkness. Jan is gone.

I try the pelican trick: lifting from my body, imagining myself above it. The girl gasping for breath on the sidewalk, her body prickling with sweat, is some other creature and I'm coasting on air currents, every flap of

my enormous wingspan propelling me farther and farther away. It works sometimes—like when Christopher
Neil has me pinned against a stack of hockey nets. But
it doesn't work now. I'm too aware of the clench in my
chest. The raw ache of my stomach. Panic.

I stamp my foot to call Dad back to me, but maybe
there's some other noise competing with my own. Or
maybe Dad and Jan are just too far away to hear. Maybe
Dad checked into the hotel already. Maybe Jan wandered somewhere, thinking I was with him. Maybe it
will be hours before they realize I'm missing. Morning.
I stamp again.

Then Jan's hands are in front of my face. She lowers
them and holds them there, her fingertips practically
skimming my breasts. She keeps them still, waiting.
Doesn't switch them on until my hands are wrapped
around her wrists. I can see the blur of her fingers, but the
flashes of light behind her are distracting. There's *hotel*.
Maybe *bus*. She must know I can't understand, because
she tries to slip her hands under my palms, yet another
attempt at hand-over-hand. But I'm not blind yet, and
that's one thing she can't make me do.

When Dad's hand touches my arm, I grab at him to
pull him close, then press my head against his chest. *Carry
me*, I sign. Then again: *carry me, carry me*. He can see my
fingers even though I can't, but he still doesn't bend to
lift me.

I cup my palm to his neck and feel the hum of words.
He's talking to Jan. Probably just agreeing as she insists

I be more independent. That I'm too old to be carried. That we should have brought the cane. Him saying she's right, she's always right.

I told Jan if she brought the cane I'd hit someone with it. She signed, *You will get used to it, Karen.* So I clarified: I would hit someone on purpose. I didn't specify her, but of course that's what I meant. *I don't need it,* I told her.

And in Fort Smith, I don't need it. When the sun is down, the only light is the soft glow of house windows. Dad beams the flashlight at my chest then on the ground, showing me where to walk. That's one Jan technique I have grudgingly accepted as useful.

Now Dad turns so his back is against my stomach, takes my hand, and places it on his shoulder. I leap up, hugging his waist with my knees, then close my eyes.

Maybe most twelve-year-olds don't ride piggyback on their dads, but it's not like I'm otherwise blending in with most twelve-year-olds. It's not like this is the solitary difference that keeps me from being normal. Normal girls can hear. They're not on a collision course to blindness, hurtling towards a predictable outcome with no predictable time frame. Next year, maybe. Next week.

Jan says it's not like that; it's a gradual thing. Night vision first — check. Then my peripheral vision will reduce until it's like I'm peering through a toilet paper roll — check again. What's yet to come: the toilet paper roll will shrink in diameter until it resembles a straw — first

the regular type and then the juice-box type. And then—
ta-da!—there might as well be marbles in my eye sockets.
At least I won't need my glasses.

I'm supposed to believe everything Jan says because
she's an expert in other people's misery. Because her dad
has Usher Syndrome, but Usher "III," not "I" like me.
Which means he just glided towards blindness at a lei-
surely pace. Didn't arrive until after he was fifty. There's
a lot of seeing a person can do in fifty years. Excuse me
for not being sympathetic.

Jan's dad is just as deaf as me, though. *Just as* meaning:
completely. So's her mom. Jan is the perfectly abled prod-
uct of a disabled union who has decided to use her boundless capabilities for good—and my dad's paycheque. Jan
says: not *dis*-abled, *differently* abled. She spells *deaf* with a
capital *D*. She claims her first language was ASL. Good for
her. What I say: at least Anne Sullivan was blind and had
some actual authority on the subject. But I guess I'm not
exactly Helen Keller, either. As my father likes to remind
me, she was a keen pupil.

In the hotel room, Dad sits on the edge of his bed, and I
sit on the edge of mine. Our knees touch. Even without
my hands on his wrists, he keeps his fingers right in the
centre of my field of vision. My eyes ache from the lights
outside, but now at least I can see.

*Are you hungry? Do you want to watch the fireworks?
Should we go to the Falls?*

Niagara was my idea, and I don't want to leave the hotel room. Not at night, anyways. Jan predicted it would be overwhelming: all the people, flashing neon everywhere. It might be hard to navigate, she told me. Which was the closest she got to disapproving any of my ideas.

She didn't need to come. I told Dad that. When Mr. Bourke started his collection—the jar in the Legion, the one at the Northern, the rummage sale in the high school gymnasium—the intention was a trip for Dad and me. There was no Jan then, and we had managed. We'd been managing ever since I was six months old and we moved to Edmonton without my mom. Managed in Edmonton, then managed when we moved back to Smith, my mom living in Hay River with Trevor by then, her hands as slow and stupid as ever.

Just us, right, I had signed to Dad.

Maybe, Karen.

And the next morning it was Jan said this, and Jan said that, the verdict decided without me.

At least she's in her own room. Or was, because the blur of her is approaching now. She settles on the bed beside Dad and it's nauseating how identically they're dressed, both of them in black, long-sleeve shirts it's way too hot for. Another Jan idea—so that when they sign, their hands stand out against their clothes. No more plaid button-downs for Dad. No more Led Zeppelin concert Ts. Instead, they match like a married couple.

Jan's put on her running shoes, which means we're going out.

And I suppose we have to. Because guaranteed there will be an article in the *Slave River Journal* with our vacation pictures, beside the thank-you letter I'll be forced to write about how blessed I am to have seen someplace outside of Smith before I can no longer see anything at all. I can't just write about the hotel room, which we had to skimp on to afford Niagara in the high season, to cover two rooms instead of one. There is no air conditioner, only a slow ceiling fan, and it's as hot inside as out.

The day Jan arrived was the third time I met Christopher Neil in the equipment room during lunch recess, the time I realized he expected more than kisses. After I had scrubbed the tears off my face at the janitor's sink, I endured an entire afternoon with him sitting two rows over, one row back. I felt his eyes sliding over my back that whole time, slipping under my bra straps, despite the fact that whenever I turned, he wasn't looking.

After school, I walked home with Mrs. Bourke like usual—because she lives three doors down and because Dad says if I don't, he'll pick me up himself. All I wanted was to be in my room, buried under my covers, but when we got to the house, Mrs. Bourke didn't wave goodbye. Instead, she cut up the driveway and I had to follow behind her. Then Dad opened the door and there was Jan beside him, beaming.

I hadn't forgotten she was coming. How could I have?

She was all Dad had been talking about since he hired her: hand-over-hand signing, Braille, hand-over-hand signing, canes, hand-over-hand signing. Like I should have been equally thrilled. Like I should have longed for my blindness to arrive even sooner so as to test the new skills I was bound to master. I'd been thinking about Jan all morning. Dreading her. But when Christopher Neil slipped his hand under my T-shirt, he'd given me something worse to dread. Thoughts of Jan had been erased.

This is Jan, Dad signed to me, to Mrs. Bourke, trapping us both in the doorway.

And I had stood silent and let Mrs. Bourke fawn over Jan. It was obvious she was, her mouth flapping, her eyes all crinkled. Mrs. Bourke has never gotten the hang of total communication. Mrs. Bourke is not even that skilled at sign, and has mostly abandoned her binder of photocopied sign dictionaries for the ease of explaining things with paper and pen. Dad doesn't know that and I won't tell him, because I like Mrs. Bourke. She knows when to give me space, for one thing. She knows that every single moment doesn't have to be a teachable moment. Which is more than I can say for my father.

And then Mrs. Bourke left. Dad closed the door behind her and I burst into tears.

Dad's face was panicky, but Jan just kept smiling. She turned to Dad and he nodded, and nodded, and then he backed out of the room.

I remember how scared I was when my dad was going blind, and how scared he was too, Jan said. *But life is a lot less scary when you learn to take control of things yourself. That's what I'm here to help with.*

She began in ASL, then backtracked and repeated herself in Signed English. Her mouth stayed closed. The sentiment was fine; mostly I was startled by how she looked. She was younger than I expected, for one thing. There was a streak of purple in her hair. Her left ear was pierced in three places. Her breasts were exactly what I wished mine were: non-existent. I could have thanked her, but instead I signed: *Dad believes in total communication. You are supposed to talk when you sign.* And then I went into my room and slammed the door.

The next morning, I was going to apologize to her, but when I woke, she and Dad were already in the kitchen, her drinking coffee from the mug I'd given Dad the first Christmas after we moved back to Smith. She was talking and Dad was laughing. Then she started signing as she spoke, and Dad swivelled in his chair towards the doorway. When he saw me, he stood and gave me a hug, lifting my feet off the ground.

Jan says we should paint our walls navy, to contrast with our hands. Also, I should wear dark shirts. This morning she's going to sit in on your class to see if there's any advice she can give Mrs. Bourke.

I thought about Christopher Neil. Then I thought about what Dad would say if he knew how little Mrs. Bourke and I signed together. *No.*

I don't have to go today. That can wait, Gary. I hated that she used his first name.

Karen, the sooner we make the changes, the better. The faster you'll learn.

Change is hard, Jan said. *We can take things slow.*

I actually believed she meant it.

I'm hungry, and Dad says we can go to McDonald's, which is my choice because I've never tried it and because Jan says it's garbage. She only stopped being a vegetarian the week before she moved to Smith.

My cheeseburger tastes like cardboard and Dad's nuggets are only slightly better. Jan says she's not hungry, and only orders fries. Then she returns to the counter and comes back with two apple pies shaped like puffed-up Pop Tarts.

These used to be my favourite, she signs, handing one to me. It takes effort not to enjoy it.

When we leave the restaurant, I ask Dad to carry me, but he shakes his head and instead clasps my hand. Clifton Hill is thick with bodies, everyone jostling, skimming my side as they pass. All the flashing lights, the streaks of neon, make my eyes ache, and it's easier to shut them than to keep them open. Either way, I can't see my feet or anyone else on the sidewalk until either I've walked into them or Dad jerks me sideways just in time. The third time I trip, Dad lifts me onto his back. Safe there above the crowds, the smells swell into focus: car exhaust, perfume, ketchup, coconut sunscreen—a big-city summer.

Dad leans forward, stooped beneath my weight. He

grips my legs, bouncing me back onto his hips when my knees slip below. I half expect to see a tower of rock on the horizon, but there's only more slices of light. Then, as we get farther down the hill, the air turns cooler. Farther still, and it becomes damp. Then the tremor of the Falls starts in my chest.

When we reach the water, Dad crouches to set me on the ground, then takes my hands and places them on the warm railing. This is what the guidebook proclaimed to be the "unmatched beauty of the illuminated Falls at night." There's a faint red glow, then a yellow one when I shift my head, a green glow when I shift it further. Blurriness that must be water. Basically: nothing. At least Dad and Jan don't ask what I think. Or maybe they do, but I can't read the question on their hands.

We sit on the damp grass beside the path when the fireworks start, but my eyes can't see wide enough to enjoy them. I move my head side to side to scan the sky, but by the time I find the explosions, they're only dim flashes and faint drips of colour. Nothing close to the spectacle the guidebook promised. I lie down and rest my head on Dad's legs, then close my eyes, waiting for the air shudders that follow the gunpowder bursts, imagining them as something impressive. The Falls rumble in my body, but that's no different from back home, sitting beside the Slave.

We took Jan to the river at the end of April, to the

Rapids of the Drowned just outside of town. The pelicans had been back for a couple of weeks, and she wanted to see them. Jan finds everything about Smith riveting. The Kaeser's: guacamole powder, but not a single avocado, underwear an aisle away from bananas! Tinfoil on our bedroom windows! An ice road to Fort Chip! The pool in a portable! Ski-Doos! Jan, who won't eat red meat but who just couldn't resist a piece of Mr. Bourke's caribou dry meat, spread with bacon grease, because of its authenticity. But she found the pelicans most fascinating of all, and we had to freeze beside the river for hours so she could stare at them.

Despite the sun, which had turned our yard to mud, the river was covered in jagged ice. The rapids never freeze, though. Instead, they hurl ice sheets large as windowpanes at the shore. Jan skidded across the ice for a better view of the birds, but Dad's too afraid to let me near the river, ice-covered or not. We just sat on a rock and watched.

By then, Jan had been in Smith for a month and I had met Christopher in the bathroom five more times. Not because I wanted to, but because I was afraid of what he'd do if I didn't show up. That he might tell the other boys I'd been meeting him willingly. I knew that whatever story Christopher invented would become truth, because people liked him. Because, according to Mrs. Bourke, he was a charming young man. I would cease to be invisible. Instead, I'd be the slut. And I could only defend myself on a piece of paper, or by flapping my hands in a way that no one could understand but my father—the last person I wanted to find out.

Christopher's hands had touched every part of my body, and mine had touched parts of his I didn't even want to know existed. And after, when he finally left me alone, I would spit and spit and spit into the janitor's sink, then huddle beside the bags of pinnies and cry until my watch read 12:50. At which point I'd slip outside and walk around to the front doors so that when I reached them, my cheeks seemed red from wind, not tears.

Back in class, Christopher wouldn't look at me, and I wouldn't look at him. I'd continue to hate myself for my stupidity. For once believing that Christopher Neil had chosen me over all the other girls because he liked me, not because my breasts were biggest, because I couldn't tell him to stop.

That day at the rapids, I'd stared at the tunnel of sky overhead and waited for pelicans to swoop into my field of vision. When they did, I'd imagine I was with them, gliding over Smith. Untouchable. That next day at school, pushed up against the hockey nets, I'd pictured being among the pelicans again. And though I'd still felt Christopher's mean fingers, I felt them less.

My eyelids glow, which means Dad has switched on the flashlight he always carries at night. When I open my eyes, his fingers blur in the thin beam that points towards me. I shake my head and he moves his hands so close to my face I'm overpowered by the lavender of hotel soap. If I concentrated, I could probably read his words, but I don't want to. I don't want to talk to Dad about the fireworks, about the Falls, about how much of a mistake it was to think I'd be able to appreciate something so immense when I can only see slivers of things at a time. I close my eyes. *I can't understand*, I sign. *I can't see your fingers.*

Dad lifts my head off his leg and sets it on the grass. When I feel his body shift, I sit up and my eyes are finally in the right place: a spiral of blue bursts open the sky in front of me, then collapses into a shower of silver. Shooting colour fills my entire vision. There's an explosion of green, then yellow, then red as the ground shudders.

When it fades to darkness, I turn to Dad, but all that's visible beside me are deep creases where the shadows overlap. Jan points the flashlight towards me. *Your father just needs some time by himself*, she signs in the beam.

Jan is too weak to carry me, and I wouldn't want her to anyways. Still, it's even darker now and I have to walk with one hand outstretched so I don't bump into anything or anyone. It takes forever to get back to the hotel, and Dad's not in the room. I know as soon as we open the door, even before the light is switched on. I can feel the emptiness.

Where is he? I ask.

Don't worry, she signs back. *He'll be back soon.*

How do you know? The plan for this trip was not for Dad to pawn me off on Jan. Does he want me to write about this in the *Slave River Journal*?

All this is tough for your dad too, Karen. There's a reason he's pushing you to learn hand-over-hand.

Because he's afraid when I'm blind we won't be able to talk to each other at all, that's what Jan means. But that's way more a problem for me than it is for Dad. At least he'll know where I am just by looking. At least he'll be able to find someone else to talk to. At least he can storm away from me to pout and not walk into traffic, not get lost on his way back to the hotel.

I'm not blind yet, I sign. Not: How am I supposed to read with my skin? How can he expect me to master the impossible? How can you?

You should get ready for bed, Jan signs. *It's late.*

I swing the door open. *You can leave*, I sign. I don't want her to; I don't want to be alone. But even more than that, I want to remind Jan that I don't need a babysitter. I'm almost a teenager. Plus, so long as the light is on, I can see fine. Well enough to manage in a room no bigger than my bedroom at home.

She closes the door: *I'll stay until your dad comes back.*

I cross the room to my suitcase without looking at her. Then I rifle through it for my pyjamas and carry them into the bathroom along with the little purse of miniature toiletries my mother sent from Hay River—her piddling contribution. When I'm done, Jan is lying on top of Dad's bed with her arms crossed over her face, but once I slip

under the covers, she stands and switches off the lights. I
don't take my glasses off.

I turn in bed so that I can see her, but of course I can't
see anything. I wouldn't know if she left the room, and
she's fully aware of that, so there's nothing to make her
stay. I feel around the bedside table for the flashlight, then
clutch it to my chest. I keep my eyes open and facing the
door. If Jan left, or if Dad came in, I'd likely notice the
hall light when the door opened.

I kick off the covers so the slow breeze from the fan
skims my bare arms and legs. When I'm blind, even the
hall light wouldn't be visible. Dad could return and sit
on my bed and he'd be as lost to me as if he were halfway around the world. Lost forever, because unless he
reached out to touch me, I'd never know he was there. I
should have tried harder to read his hands. I should have
answered him.

I switch on my flashlight and aim the beam at the
other bed. Jan is faced away from me, but when I pull the
cord on the bedside lamp, she sits up.

It's late, Karen, she signs, then yanks the cord again.

I keep my eyes towards the door and count backwards
from a hundred. If Dad returns before I reach one, I'll be
able to see for three more years, I tell myself. Then I start
again: two more years. And again: one more year. And
again: eleven more months. And again.

I beam the flashlight at Jan's back, then stand and lean
over her. Her eyes are closed and her shoulders rise and
fall steadily. There's a television against the opposite wall,

and I click it on, then quickly press Mute. Crouched a foot away from the screen, I flip through the channels, but there's no closed-captioning, only scrolling news on CNN. I lie back down with the remote on my chest and keep flipping, but everything is blurred. Better company than darkness, at least.

I don't mind being alone when it's light out. I'm used to it. At recess, Mrs. Bourke goes to the staff room and I just walk loops around the school. I can't exactly skip rope or play soccer. I can't exactly talk to anyone. Sometimes kids in the younger grades come up and sign: *Hello, what's your name?* As if they don't know. And then: *My name is* followed by some awkward finger-spelling. All the classes have learned some sign, thanks to my father. Every year he gives worksheets to the secretary to "support my inclusion."

It was a month after Christopher transferred to our school that he bumped into me near the basketball court. I brought my fist to my chest to sign *sorry*, but he grabbed my hand mid-rotation and tucked a piece of paper into my palm. Then he took off. I opened the paper: *Meet me in the gym.*

I had felt his eyes on me before, but I assumed it was because of how weird I seemed: hunched in my desk beside Mrs. Bourke, every so often my hands flapping at her. My thick glasses. The other girls always smiling at me and waving, always careful to sign hello but rarely anything beyond that. Like I was the class pet, and not the only one of them who'd gotten perfect on every math test that year. But reading that note, I thought: *Maybe he likes me.* A burst of heat detonated in my stomach and shot outwards until my legs felt loose and my hands quivered.

The gym door was propped open, and when I pushed inside, Christopher was right there. It was dark, but I could see the glow of the equipment room, which was where he pulled me, my hand slick in his. *You're pretty,* he signed. *K-A-R-E-N.* His fingers were slow when he signed, but quick when they grabbed my face and pulled it towards his. He pushed his tongue into my mouth. I couldn't breathe, but it didn't matter. When he stepped away, my lips felt numb. *Thank you,* he signed, and slipped out the door. I sat down and leaned against a bag of basketballs, my cheeks still hot where his hands had pressed. *He does like me,* I thought. *He thinks I'm pretty.* When I made my way back into class, recess was over, but Mrs. Bourke believed me that I'd been in the bathroom. I glanced at Christopher and his eyes were on his desk.

Sometimes I try to relive that first time in my mind, blocking out all the times that came afterwards. I try to remember the feeling of being wanted by a boy I liked. And I liked Christopher. Or at least, I liked that he was different from the other boys. Taller, with hair past his ears—like my dad's in pictures from before I was born. And always a book on his desk—a novel, and never one assigned for school. In class, the other girls circled him like hawks. They still do.

I am wide awake when the light switches on. I sit up, expecting to see Dad at the door, but instead Jan is striding towards the television set. She turns it off.

She sits on the edge of my bed and swivels to face me, then puts her hands out in front of her. She's staring at me with her mouth twisted up, and I don't want to touch her wrists. I keep my eyes on the sheets—build and topple mountains with my knees. Jan puts two fingers on my chin and pulls my gaze up.

Did you see what was on the television? she signs.

I could tell her the truth—I saw nothing—but from the look on her face I can guess what was on. I skimmed through at least three channels of it. And a lecture from Jan is better than lying in the dark, alone, convincing myself Dad will never come back. I finger-spell: *Pornography.*

Jan takes a deep breath and shakes her head. *Karen, pornography is not appropriate for someone your age.* I shift my eyes down and she chin-taps my face up again. *If you're curious about sex, Karen, you can ask me any questions you have. But what you were watching is not an accurate representation.*

I know what's accurate, I sign. *Just because I'm deaf doesn't mean I've never done anything.*

I glance up at Jan's face to check her reaction. Her mouth flaps open, but her hands stay still in her lap. Then she brings them to her temples and rubs circles with her fingertips. I bite away my smile.

You're too young for a boyfriend, Jan signs finally. *You should enjoy your childhood.*

I don't have a boyfriend, I tell her. *But I'm not a child.*

Jan's body softens. She smiles at me. *You're right, Karen, you're not a child. And you will have those experiences when you're ready.*

I have those experiences now. With Christopher—I spell out his name because without that it's only a story.

What experiences? Jan asks.

I shrug. *Practically everything.* It's a lie, but what does that matter?

Her eyes are wide, and before her hands lift again I add: *Life is less scary when you take control.* She doesn't seem to recognize her own platitude. Her fingers move at rapid speed, only partially in view.

I close my eyes to them, take my glasses off, then lie back down. I can still feel Jan's weight on the edge of the bed, her eyes glued to my face. Sleep comes quickly.

When I wake, I know Dad is back because I smell his shaving cream. I also know that telling Jan about Christopher was a major mistake. Shocking Jan is hardly worth the interrogation I am sure to get from my father. Hardly worth whatever he will do once we get back to Smith—to Christopher, to Mrs. Bourke, to me. There are still two weeks of school left.

When I roll over and open my eyes, Dad is sitting on the edge of his bed watching me. He's already dressed. The blinds are drawn still, but the room is bright.

Good morning, Karen, he signs.

I put on my glasses and glance around the room, but it's just us. Then I pull the clock on the bedside table towards me: 8:58 — only seven o'clock Smith time. Jan must still be asleep.

Get ready and we'll have breakfast, he signs.

Dad's lips are a tight line and his eyes look swollen, but he doesn't bring up Christopher. Maybe Jan didn't tell him. Maybe this is still about his hands at the fireworks.

I rummage in my suitcase for a pair of shorts and a T-shirt. Dad doesn't move from the edge of his bed. He just stares at his hands, folded in his lap. When I open my toiletries to pull out my toothbrush, out falls a folded square of paper. The words inside are in Jan's tight script: *Your father needs to know about that boy. I'll let you tell him yourself. Today.*

There was a sign for breakfast specials two doors down, Dad signs when we get into the lobby.

Where's Jan? I ask.

I thought this morning it could just be us two. We'll meet Jan later.

Clearly, Jan arranged this. My opportunity to tell my father a boy has put his hand under my bra, inside my underwear.

At the restaurant, Dad slides into the booth across from me. He keeps his eyes on me while I read the menu. I don't feel like eating but ask for pancakes, and he orders some from the waitress.

Jan can't make me tell Dad about Christopher. Not today, anyways. I'll promise to tell him when we're home. Say it's not fair to make me ruin the holiday. Or maybe I'll just say I lied.

Are we going to the Falls after? I ask. In daylight it will be better. Maybe if I move my head fast from left to right, my mind will stitch the slices together into a complete view.

Dad just stares at me. Then he stretches out his hands until they're across the table and waits for me to take his wrists. *Jan says there's something you need to talk to me about.*

Of course she said something already. I cross my arms over my chest and shake my head.

Jan says there's a problem with a boy at school. Which boy?

I'm not hungry, I sign. Then I get up from the booth and try to navigate my way to the exit, bumping elbows and tripping over legs.

Dad follows after me, grabs my shoulder just as I reach the door, and turns me towards him. *You can tell me later. You need to eat.* I don't argue. I just follow him back to the table, keep my eyes on my food and my grip tight on my cutlery.

Dad and I walk side by side to the top of the Falls, the wide stretch of water before it plummets down the rocks. He doesn't try to carry me, and I don't ask. He holds my elbow instead of my hand.

The view is clearer than last night, but not by much. What did I expect—my vision stretching to encompass something this enormous? A miracle?

Other than Smith, this is the last place I'll see. I want to take it back. I want to be beside the ocean, in a rainforest, waiting for whales or bears. I want to be in the Rockies, or touring Parliament Hill, or walking through Green Gables. But those were all Jan's ideas.

Dad steps in front of me and signs: *Do you see the rainbow?* He points through the mist to a haze of blue — sky and water blurred together.

Maybe his fear is fact: I've waited too long. The cane, the Braille, the hand-over-hand — I won't be able to learn those things before I'm blind. Dad will have to look after me forever. And though I'll be able to sign to him all I want, I won't know if he's there to see my hands, or what he wants to say in return.

The cement wall goes to my thighs, and beside me there's a boy on top of it. He's on his knees, his chest leaned against the metal railing. I climb up and stand next to him. He's younger, eight or nine. His eyes are wide and he has a huge smile on his face, because of course he sees everything: the rainbow, the waterfall, every single ripple of water, every drop of mist fogging the air in front of us. Because he's having the sort of spectacular trip I wished for.

Dad grabs my right leg just as I swing my left over the railing, straddling it. This would make a story for the *Journal*. This would make a story for the world: DEAF BLIND GIRL JUMPS OVER NIAGARA FALLS. I wonder if Christopher would be impressed. Or would he be ashamed of himself, thinking he had something to do with it? Don't flatter yourself, Christopher.

Dad wraps his arms around me, his fingers digging into my legs. In 1960, a seven-year-old boy went over the Falls in only a life jacket. He lived. But it's already been established: miracles don't happen to me.

The boy beside me shifts, and when I glance at him, his fingers are moving. I turn to his mom and hers are moving back. Out of the hundreds of people watching the Falls at this very moment, beside me is the only other deaf kid I've ever seen. Which may be a coincidence, or may mean Dad steered me to this spot to orchestrate some kind of disabled-child convention. I try to resist, but can't: *Are you deaf?* I sign.

The boy thrusts his hands out and pinches the air between our faces with his thumbs and index fingers. It's ASL, but I understand: *What are you doing?* He points to my legs, straddling the fence. Then he signs *not, scared, you,* his face shaped in a question.

Life is less scary when you take control, I tell him.

His mom pulls him down and then leans up against the fence beside me. She touches my arm, then stacks her hands, each one forming a *K.* She rotates them in front of her chest. *Careful.* When I don't respond, she moves them forward and up until they're almost skimming my face. Dad clutches me even tighter.

I close my eyes and imagine I'm a pelican, my feathers rippling in the gusts of cool air churned by the waterfall. Birds regularly get swept down the Falls, particularly in foggy weather, but even more of them pass right over,

coasting on air currents. I stretch out my arms, feel the
mist on my pelican wings. Then I lift up, above it all.

SECOND COMINGS AND GOINGS

We all knew of the boy before he moved into the basement of Grace Lutheran Church. Many of us were fans of the rock musician who discovered him playing outside the Bratislava train station, and had gone to the McPherson Theatre to see the final performance of the boy's cross-Canada tour. We were impressed with his fingers—*fast as lightning*, we said—and the way he leapt and danced as his bow flew over the strings of his violin. We felt privileged to hear authentic gypsy music, though some of us referred to the boy as a Roma, which we knew to be the correct term.

The day after the concert, we saw him again, on the six o'clock news. *Nine-year-old virtuoso suffers devastating blow*, the news anchor's voice-over proclaimed. On screen, the child's robe-clad mother was slumped on the floor in the lobby of Paul's Motor Inn. There was a close-up shot of her vacant stare, her red-rimmed eyes, and then the camera panned to the boy, the reporter's thick hand on his arm. The child announced that he had received a long-distance phone call the night before. While we watched him perform onstage, halfway across the world his little wooden house in Slovakia had been set ablaze, and his father and five sisters, who were sleeping at the time, had been *burnt to cinders*.

In the days following this announcement, we watched the demonstrations play out on our television sets. We saw the UVic branch of the International Socialists, together with the Raging Grannies, set up camp on the lawn of El Rancho Restaurant. (There being no Slovak consul-ate in our city, the Socialists declared that El Rancho—with its vast menu of entrées from the neighbouring Czech Republic—was the most suitable location.) To decry eastern Europe's treatment of her wandering sons and daughters, the demonstrators smeared *smažený sýr* on windows of cars in the restaurant parking lot, then dropped a match on the stolen takeout menus piled on the front lawn (not just from El Rancho, but from Rathskeller Schnitzel House and Cook 'N Pan, the Polish deli, and, when the blaze began to die out, Ali Baba Pizza and Ming's Chinese).

"Hell no," the protesters shouted later—after the insti-gators of what was, by then, referred to as the El Rancho Inferno had been released on bail and the government had turned down the boy and his mother's request for refugee status. "Hell no, don't make them go." It was January, and they were on the lawn of the Legislature, dancing in circles in the mud around the fountain in head scarves and long skirts, beaded shawls and heavy eyeliner (their standard garb, or clothes chosen in solidarity with the gypsy family? We debated it, but came to no certain conclusions).

Shown a picture of the boy then, any of us would have recognized him: a nest of thick hair, wolf eyes, limbs like sticks. But to us he was just the violin boy, that gypsy kid — the miracles hadn't yet begun.

They didn't start until days after Sunday service on February 15, when Angus McCarthy approached Pastor Neil and, after touching his shoulder to get his attention, produced a square of newsprint from the front pocket of his button-down cotton shirt. The clipping was a story about the boy's upcoming deportation. *Haven't we, as Christians,* Angus asked, *a responsibility to help this boy in the name of the Lord? And isn't it a fact,* he continued, *that the Sunday school room in the basement — with its plush rugs and beaded mobiles, its 3-D Christ fastened to the wall with screws — has a hot plate, a fridge, a sink, a toilet, all unused for six days of every week?*

Some of us, overhearing the conversation, suspected that Angus's interest in charity had a great deal to do with convincing his own wife and daughter (do-gooders, but disbelievers) to return to our dwindling flock. Nevertheless, no one could dispute that the idea was a good one. Offering sanctuary to a mother and her child was a gesture of goodwill that would make the Lord, and the community, take notice. And though we had had the occasional problem with mice in the basement, as well as with mould and leaking pipes, the Son of God Himself had lived with less. So that evening, when the Reverend placed phone calls to members of the church council, they all pledged support for the idea.

The next day, Angus McCarthy's daughter Judy contacted an acquaintance whose boyfriend was the bass player for the local flamenco band the Flaming Gypsies. The band members were not, in fact, Roma, but were rumoured to be harbouring the boy and his mother in an apartment building on Michigan Street. At four o'clock Monday afternoon, Judy arrived at the church in Angus's white Tercel, the boy and his mother in the back. Many of us were on the lawn waiting with yogurt containers of chicken noodle soup or bags of hand-me-down clothing. Doug and Barb Portus brought two mattresses in the back of their pickup truck, as well as the dismantled frame of a bunk bed that had been their grandson's. While the men put the bed together in the Sunday school room, the women filled the fridge and gave the boy and his mother an official Grace Lutheran tour.

Joyce Ennis

Grace Lutheran used to be a dying congregation. There were only about thirty of us who attended on a regular basis, not counting children, and everyone I knew was thinking about leaving. One Sunday, Danny went to Grace and I took the

kids to Hope Lutheran on Carrick Street. We saw
the Pauls and Pattersons there, the Mendels and
Marconis. Hope Lutheran had a summer day camp,
a youth service group, family movie nights, a Bible
study with more than five members. It had a choir,
and I love to sing. But Danny was Grace's treasurer
and he wouldn't abandon his post. The next week
I went back.

Pastor Neil asked Danny for advice about taking
the boy in. Danny's response: too much work and
not enough congregants to share it between. But he
was looking at the situation as an accountant, not
as a father, and when I called Pastor Neil at home,
I told him as much. *What*, I asked, *would Jesus do?*
I was certain that with the boy around, the others
would come back.

THE MIRACLES

The miracles started the day after the boy arrived, when
ten-year-old Sylvie Mann was sitting alone in the church
parking lot, in the back seat of the family minivan. While
waiting for her parents to deliver a ground beef casser-
ole to the boy and his mother, Sylvie saw the holly bush
by the stairs burst into flames, forming a smoke cloud
that bore a striking resemblance to a certain hammer-
swinging carpenter. Sylvie Mann is known to have an
overactive imagination, and had, in fact, just learned the

story of the Burning Bush in Sunday school the week before. For these reasons, her parents thought little of the tale and, after inspecting the bush for signs of fire damage, chastised her by reciting the eighth commandment: Thou Shall Not Bear False Witness.

Denise Nguyen came to the church on Wednesday night to pray for her sister, who was scheduled for a hip replacement the next morning at the Royal Jubilee Hospital. She looked up from her Bible when some movement on the wall behind the alter caught her eye, and saw the plaster Jesus smile at her, wink, then point a finger towards the boy—who was sitting in a back pew with a shoebox full of comic books given to him by Justin Morash's family. There were others in the church at the time, but as no one else appeared to notice the moving statue, Denise attributed the vision to stress, and stopped at Shoppers Drug Mart on her way home to purchase lavender-scented aromatherapy bath salts and a bottle of B-complex vitamins.

On Thursday, Winnie Calder baked oatmeal raisin cookies for the Bible study group, but burned the second batch and left her house with the tin only half full. She placed the tin at the centre of the table, and it appeared that most people took at least one cookie—with Harry Nguyen grabbing six or seven. Still, at the end of the evening, there were enough left to pack in her children's lunches. But even this event was not taken to be a miracle at first. Winnie simply assumed that the church members did not appreciate her baking, and had only pretended to take the cookies, or had perhaps taken them and then put them back when she wasn't looking.

Between 10 p.m. Friday night and 6 a.m. Saturday morning, the letters on the church's sign were rearranged from WELCOME Y.M.I. PEACE GIRLS (in honour of the young women showing slides of war-torn Africa to audiences at Alix Goolden Performance Hall) to WELCOME GYPSIE MIRACLE. But those of us who saw the sign, or heard about it, assumed it to be the work of drunken teenagers (who had been caught altering the sign in the past, spelling out GOD IS DEAD, and WORSHIP PUSSY).

The undisputed miracle occurred on that first Sunday, when the boy and his mother had been living in the church for just under a week. During Sunday school, Angelina De Mar, a precocious four-year-old, laid her head on the table and complained of feeling dizzy. When Barb Portus, the Sunday school teacher, placed her hand on the child's forehead, she said it was like touching an oven door. Barb took the stairs two by two on her way to notify Angelina's parents. But when Mr. De Mar ran down to the basement, he found his daughter leaping across the carpet with the other children, the boy serenading them on his violin. Angelina's skin was cool to the touch, and when asked if she still felt unwell, she announced that the boy had cured her.

Justin Morash

Yeah, I was there for the so-called miraculous healing. I'm probably the only fifteen-year-old on earth who's forced to spend Sunday mornings making beaded Noah's ark mobiles and Bible bookmarks. Sitting "criss-cross apple sauce" with a bunch of kindergartners while Mrs. Portus thrills us with Bible stories and tests our retention skills. *Come on, children, let me see you draw Esau and the priciest bowl of soup.*

Angelina didn't feel like colouring in Joseph's dream coat, so all of a sudden she's too dizzy to hold her crayons. She makes one weak attempt at a whimper, and Mrs. Portus flips. Because if her precious favourite loses interest in Our Lord, it means the world is ending.

Angelina is a spoiled brat. If I were hospitalized, my parents would wheel me to church on a gurney. They practically did, when I was seven and had chicken pox. I passed it on to half the Sunday school class. But if Angelina even has a runny nose, she stays home watching cartoons. And when she comes back, she's without fail the special helper, mixing up tempura paint while Mrs. Portus leads the rest of us in rousing musical tributes to Jesus, our asses freezing off on the concrete floor.

After Mrs. Portus left the room, the boy whispered something in Angelina's ear. Maybe that he knew she was faking. And the next minute he has his violin out and she's dancing around. If you want to call it something, call it what it is. Bullshit.

THE ANNOUNCEMENT

Mrs. Edith Stone, the church organist and council secretary and a long-time member of the congregation, was the first to call the healing of Angelina De Mar what it was: a miracle. It was after Sunday service, and we were gathered in the church hall for fellowship and Nanaimo bars, listening to Barb Portus's account of the event. As the other miracles were recounted — the burning holly bush, the winking Christ, the multiplying cookies, the rearranged sign — the flushed circles that dotted the centre of each of Mrs. Stone's cheeks spread outwards until they reached her ears. *Could it be*, she asked, *that the Second Coming has arrived in Victoria, British Columbia, on the doorstep of Grace Lutheran Church?*

There were many among us who had been thinking this exact thought. It seemed likely, yes, that the child had been a test for our congregation. He was persecuted, homeless, and had we not rescued him? Had we not provided shelter? While we were discussing these matters, the boy was racing through the mud puddles on the front lawn, playing tag with Angelina and her friends. His limbs were not sticks after all, but long and graceful as an elk's. His hair not an untamed nest, but a shining tousle of curls.

It was a wonder we hadn't noticed this perfection earlier.

Mrs. Stone was the one who made the proposal: in-depth religious training for the child, under the council's tutelage. We would contact the government and alert the media only when the Second Coming was ready. Those of us deemed loyal enough to share our opinions all agreed with this course of action. As for the rest of us, a handful of first-timers who had attended to catch a glimpse of the boy, the council determined we needed time to prove our faith.

Tony Hendricks

The first time I went to Grace Lutheran was Miracle Sunday. I'd never been particularly religious, but my parents are, and I went to Holy Cross Lutheran in Winnipeg when I was growing up.

My mom was always sending emails with Victoria church listings. A place to meet a nice girl, she said. Cindy, my brother's wife, went to Sunday school with us at Holy Cross. A prize heifer if she's a prize at all, but at least she loves Jesus.

Anyways, that Saturday night I'd met some buddies at Garrick's Head Pub. Brad was there — the drummer for the Flaming Gypsies. He was like, man, those gypsies, they're living in some Lutheran church. I said I'd been Lutheran growing up, so he asked me to come with him and check the place out. He was afraid to go alone and be forced to take Communion or something. So we went, and the Reverend made this sermon about Mary and Joseph wandering through Bethlehem and no one offering them a place to stay. Which was more of a Christmas sermon, really, but fitting, I guess, because of the gypsies. And then after about half an hour someone ran up the aisle and whispered something to the Reverend. He wrapped things up pretty quickly after that.

I didn't want to stay, but Brad was my ride, and he wandered off to talk to the gypsy woman. I got a coffee and was pretending to read the bulletin board, waiting for him, when the miracle was announced. People will tell you they were skeptical, but that's a lie. Everyone believed, right from the beginning.

THE INSTRUCTION

Although only the Reverend, the council, the child, and the Lord Himself can be certain of what occurred during the boy's religious instruction, there are a number of things the rest of us can attest to:

1. Six days a week, at precisely 8 a.m., the Reverend's station wagon pulled into the Grace Lutheran parking lot. When Pastor Neil turned off the ignition,

he went around to the passenger side to open the door for Edith Stone, and the two of them entered the church together.

2. Throughout the day, each of the nine additional council members arrived at the church for their one-hour blocks of instruction: at nine, Angus McCarthy; at ten, Danny Ennis; at eleven, Winnie Calder; at twelve, Harry Nguyen; at one, Doug Portus; at two, Sally Mann; and at three, Andy De Mar and the Morashes. The members were observed carrying a variety of items, paid for with church funds. A brief list of these instructional materials: two goldfish, a turtle-shaped kiddie pool, eight loaves of Wonder bread, and five feet of plastic tubing.

3. Each lesson day at 4:10 p.m., Pastor Neil and Edith Stone left the church. (A number of us inquired about the purpose of Edith's constant presence, and to these queries the Reverend always replied that Mrs. Stone was a fellow musician, and therefore a comfort to the boy. Aside from this, of course, she was a retired widow with plenty of free time and a tendency to push her nose into other people's business.)

4. The mother was not always present during the boy's instruction. Many of us who stopped by the

church during the daytime came across her dusting the pulpit, washing the windows, or sitting in the front pew with a Walkman on, listening to *English Made Easy!* instructional cassettes.

5. During the boy's lessons, the curtains that covered the Sunday school room's windows were drawn, and the door was closed.

Hetty Grandin

The Ennises are neighbours of ours. Our kids have played together since they were toddlers. I always knew they were religious people; each Christmas, Danny erects a Nativity scene in their front yard— enormous wooden cut-outs of Wise Men, lopsided angels hanging from the oak tree. But other than that, they're pretty quiet about their beliefs.

When the miracles happened, it was their daughter, Moira, who told my kids. I found it funny how seriously my two took it, since Ethan was a staunch atheist before all this and I was agnostic, at most. And here were our kids proclaiming the Second Coming. Next time I saw Joyce in the yard, I mentioned what Moira had said—*kids and their wild imaginations*. But Joyce said no one had imagined anything. It was true.

When I told Ethan that night, I meant to give him a laugh, not another radio idea. If I'd known he'd want to sneak the voice recorder into church, I would have kept Joyce's revelation to myself. We went to Grace Lutheran every Sunday after that.

THE CLAIM

By the time the boy's instruction was considered complete, we had multiplied tenfold. There weren't enough pews to hold us during Sunday service; we spilled into the aisle, packed the back of the room, perched on laps. Those of us who were soccer moms came armed with our equipment: folding stools with thin aluminum legs, or collapsible chairs complete with mesh drink-holders in the armrests.

Among our ranks were Catholics and Protestants, Jews and Muslims, Confucians, Rastafarians, Wiccans, and a large number of lapsed atheists. We encompassed such a range of skin tones and hair colours that passersby who didn't know better might have assumed that Grace Lutheran held weekly auditions for those United Colors of Benetton commercials.

But more had changed at the church than the size of the congregation. The Flaming Gypsies had devoted themselves to the study of worship music, and with the boy on violin, they replaced Mrs. Stone as Grace Lutheran's musical accompanist. Mrs. Stone served instead as the self-appointed mouthpiece of the council and the gypsy family. During services, she held whispered interviews with reporters who snuck into the church despite the Reverend's media ban.

What hadn't changed was the miracle tally. Though we dragged our ill and injured before the boy, he cured none of them. Not Paul Hammerstein of his chronic nosebleeds, or Ella Porter of her bunions, not Gordon Bruce's foul-mouthed grandson who the Bruces claimed was emotionally disturbed. Our elderly did not rise from their wheelchairs or toss away their canes, and Juanita Flores's cancer did not go into remission, nor—as she had hoped—did her hair grow back quicker, fuller, and with more natural curl. In fact, after Angelina's healing, the boy did nothing of note, and as the miracles were what had drawn most of us to the church in the first place, we were getting impatient.

Perhaps the council sensed this, because on March 21 the Reverend informed us there would be a meeting in the fellowship hall after service. As soon as the final hymn was sung, we descended on the refreshment tables laden with Thrifty's shortbread and misshapen Rice Krispies squares, whispering amongst ourselves about the possible purposes for such a gathering. The boy and his mother did not join us; they went downstairs to their room.

Some of us were certain the council would finally announce the results of their religious education: had they or had they not confirmed the boy's connection to the Lord? Others argued that surely it was too early to tell, and that we would only be provided with an update. Perhaps, some suggested, the council had hit a wall, had run out of instructional ideas. Perhaps they wanted input from the rest of us.

They let us speculate. The council stayed sequestered in the Reverend's office for an hour after service, where they were overheard conversing in hushed voices. When they emerged, even the packages of imitation coffee creamer had been devoured, and we were growing restless.

Mrs. Stone led the council into the hall. Under her arm, she carried a rolled poster, which she unfurled, shaking out its curl with a snap. She attached the poster to the wall with pieces of masking tape, then stood to the side, rested her hands on the wide berth of her hips, and smiled widely.

Jesus Christ stared down at us, His feet hovering above the waters of the Sea of Galilee, His arms outstretched. We were perplexed. What relevance did the poster have to our current situation? Dale Miller, an electrician who had heard about the boy while fixing the wiring in the Manns' garage, was the first to speak. *Edith,* he said, *what the hell's your point?*

The council's point was simple: Jesus could walk on water, and so — they had discovered — could our gypsy child.

The room sparked with questions. How did they know? When had they seen this? What did it mean? The remaining doubters among us responded to this miracle with logic. Perhaps, they said, the long hours of lesson planning, all those spare moments devoted to the boy's education, had exhausted the council. And perhaps, as they gathered together one evening in the parking lot and watched the boy walk across the wet asphalt, some trick of light had convinced them he was standing on the surface of puddles. For one brief moment the council shared a figment of a dream. Frankly, a number of us questioned the biblical truth of Jesus' catamaranic abilities and sided secretly with the scientists: sure, He had walked across a lake, but in the winter, when a layer of ice covered the surface. No miracle that modern-day snowmobiles couldn't achieve.

But the council claimed that the water in question was not frozen, not imagined, and that the spectacle had been as clear as day. Mrs Stone had filled a kiddie pool to the brim with water, asked the child to remove his shoes and walk across it, and he had done so. They had all been witness to the miracle. From her purse, Mrs. Stone produced a blurry photograph, which was passed from sticky hand to sticky hand around the room. And though certainly such an image didn't prove anything (a pool covered in glass, the boy caught in a jump, a seamless Photoshop stitch-job), we were now believers, and so we did what we did best. We believed.

Violetta Guattari

Religion isn't really about God; it's about indoctrinating children into accepting a patriarchal culture

that is damaging to both genders, leading to the per-
petuation of inequality and violence against women.

I didn't go to Grace Lutheran because *I* thought
the boy was the next Christ. I went because *everyone else* thought he was the next Christ. As for saying I did believe: that's participatory observation, a
common method of sociological inquiry. I'd been
studying Marx's view about religion propagat-
ing the domination of the upper class. At Grace
Lutheran this was evidenced by the way the council oppressed the larger congregation, primarily
through limiting their decision-making opportun-
ities and withholding information about the boy.
Take that photograph, so obviously fraudulent.
When they passed it around, everyone believed
because they were starved for a revelation. Not
because it proved anything at all.

THE PREPARATION

Although few of us had questioned the council's role as
the boy's educators, we were less content with their position as sole witnesses of his greatest miracle to date. Did
we not all faithfully attend services, fill the collection
plate, bake Bundt cakes to share with our fellow believers, write letters to the government pleading for refugee
status for our harboured gypsies? Did we not deserve,
then, to witness a miracle ourselves?

Mrs. Stone's kiddie pool would not suffice. The boy would need to duplicate his performance on a larger scale, someplace where our entire congregation could secure a front-row seat.

Our collective vision was as follows: Good Friday, Thetis Lake, 7 a.m. The sun would rise on the boy, alone on the shore of the island in the centre of the lake. He would wear a simple white outfit: a robe, or a suit, a cape perhaps. In the lifeguard chair would perch the Reverend, a whistle raised to his lips. And after a shrieking blast of air, we'd watch from the beach as the boy glided towards us across the water. A silhouette at first, his features would become clearer as he approached the shore and entered into our embrace. His miracle performed a second time. The Second Coming.

Of course, every one of us imagined the particulars differently. We each placed ourselves centre shore, directly in the boy's path; we each saw our own friends and family surrounding us, those two or eight or fifteen individuals we telephoned after the council's announcement to breathlessly relay the news. The next morning, rumours of the boy's upcoming performance were splashed across the front page of the *Times Colonist*, were announced by morning show radio hosts, and appeared on scrolling text at the bottom of our television screens. While we grumbled about the bean-spillers in our midst, we were all guilty before God of doing what we accused others of.

There was no use dwelling on it. Instead, we had to

tweak our vision: the main beach crowded with spectators, with television crews, with government officials ready to snatch the gypsies and arrange for immediate deportation. But we could take advantage of this. We could demand charitable donations as viewing fees, plead through the national media for refugee status for the boy. Or something beyond that: holy immunity.

We split into work groups and divided the tasks: set-up and clean-up crews and general schleppers; security (including some with lifeguard training in case of copycats); equipment procurers (bleachers, a sound system, a canoe to escort the boy to the island so early birds wouldn't witness the spectacle in advance); cookie ladies to satisfy the anticipated demand at the concession stand; and an immigration liaison. Of course, the council claimed the role of visionaries; they would make all key decisions, hold all veto power, and otherwise *do as they thought fit.*

Many of our younger members suggested possible souvenirs: action figures, key chains, postcards, water bottles. In the end, we settled on T-shirts, which could be made cheaply by Dan Ives, a recent addition to our congregation, who owned the Totally Terrific T-Shirts shop at Mayfair Mall.

During our flurry of preparation, we saw little of the boy. He attended Sunday service, but instead of playing violin, he sat in the front pew, leaning against his mother. He began to suffer from a number of complaints: nausea and upset stomachs, migraine headaches, dizzy spells. He spent most of his time in his basement room, tucked in bed. We heard that he refused all visitors—the Reverend and council members included. Edith Stone still dropped in regularly, though, pushing past the boy's mother, who offered meek protests from the doorway.

Al Archibald

When I was a boy, I had a teacher who made us recite poetry in class. Wordsworth, Longfellow, Keats, Shelley: *I met a traveller from an antique land who said: "two vast and trunkless legs of stone stand in the desert..."* To this day I carry that poem with me, but the morning I was to stand at my desk and deliver it, my mind went blank. I stood there, my classmates staring at me, Mr. Withers gesturing for me to begin. I ran to the hall, where I was sick in a wastepaper basket.

Since that day, sixty-five years ago, I have witnessed incidents involving my children and grandchildren—fumbled batons in relay races, forgotten lines in school plays, failed exams. These are not measures of capacity, but evidence of stress.

I saw the boy at church the Sunday before it happened. Everyone was making final arrangements, talking in front of him. I didn't think a thing of it until I looked at his face, but the moment I did, it was like I was looking at myself, ten years old,

"Ozymandias" on the tip of my tongue. *Round the decay of that colossal wreck, boundless and bare the lone and level sands stretch far away.*

THE EVENT

On Friday, April 9, we arrived at the lake at 4 a.m., the entire congregation with the exception of the youngest children and their parents and a number of our elderly members, for whom later bus transportation had been arranged. The police who accompanied us to the beach had difficulty keeping their opinions to themselves, and there were rumours among them that immigration officials would be attending the event and would "reel in the drowned rat." Of course, we took these threats seriously, but it was not the time to dwell on them. We roped off media zones and set up spotlights and bleachers — one section reserved for Grace Lutheran members. The Flaming Gypsies hooked up the sound system and began to practise some of their newest numbers: "Water-Walking All the Way to Heaven," a and their version of the Lovin' Spoonful's "Do You Believe in Magic" (… in the Grace gypsy's heart). The latter Edith Stone quickly vetoed as an unfitting tribute to the child of Our Lord, magic being the devil's work.

The gypsy child arrived with his mother at 6 a.m., when the beach was full and the Youth Group had already sold all five hundred T-shirts — silk-screened on the front with the image from the poster Mrs. Stone had hung on the wall of the storage room, and on the back with a photograph of Thetis Lake, a picture of the boy superimposed on the surface. The police had to escort him to the canoe, clearing a path through the crowd with their bodies. People were shouting at him, shoving pens and paper into his face, throwing gifts: baggies of gingersnaps, a houseplant, a papier mâché seagull, even a pair of cotton Hanes—which we quickly disposed of. His mother stood watching with Edith Stone.

At 7 a.m., the sun began to rise and the band played their final number. By the time the Reverend climbed into the lifeguard chair, the beach was silent. He welcomed the crowd, said a prayer for the child, and then raised his whistle to his lips. After what felt to many of us like an eternity, he blew.

Sam Knight

I bought the canoe from Camp Shine and Share. They had some fibreglass Clippers donated, and advertised the old boats in the *Buy and Sell*. Fifty dollars apiece, couple of paddles thrown in. It's aluminum, nothing special. But Marguerite likes to take it when we visit her parents in Yellow Point. We paddle past the Lodge, Marguerite with her binoculars, spying on the gentry.

I'm not comfortable around children; I can

never think what to say. Marguerite knows all the
neighbour kids by name. She remembers who goes
to what school and plays on what sports teams.
We talked about having children of our own, but
that was before she got sick. We have three cats,
though. Siamese.

The boy was quiet the whole way to the island.
Alls he said to me was "Thank you" when I helped
him out of the boat. I just nodded, but then, when
I started paddling back, I called out, "Good luck,"
because it only seemed right, and because I knew
Marguerite would ask me what we talked about,
and I didn't want to tell her that we hadn't talked
at all. She says sometimes being married to the
strong silent type isn't all it's made out to be. She's
probably joking, but also she's probably right.

I paddled back to shore and I hauled the canoe
onto the beach. An aluminum canoe is indestruct-
ible; you can drag it over rocks or ram into sand-
bars and not worry about puncturing the hull. I
didn't pull the boat too far up, though, because
Marguerite whispered that I'd need it if the boy
had a change of heart. I couldn't tell, but she said
he looked frightened, and she's a pretty good judge
of that sort of thing.

THE AFTERMATH

Not all of us had had the foresight to bring binoculars, and to those of us without them, all that was visible on the island's shore was the white shimmer of the boy's robe. He didn't start towards the water when the whistle blew, but crouched on the sand with his head in his hands. Those of us who couldn't see clearly demanded details from our neighbours who could: *What was he doing? Could they see his face? What did they expect would happen next?* Some of us turned to check how the boy's mother was responding to the delay, but she was no longer where we had last seen her—standing with Mrs. Stone at the edge of the crowd. Edith now leaned against the Reverend's lifeguard chair, and the gypsy woman was nowhere in sight.

From somewhere near the concession stand, a child began chanting the boy's name; perhaps it was Angelina De Mar. The chant grew louder and more frenzied as the rest of us joined in. We clapped our hands and stomped our feet. And after the Flaming Gypsies started a drum roll, the boy stood up and began to walk. First to the edge of the water, and then onto the lake. One, two, three, four, five steps he took across the surface. Even those of us who believed with certainty that the boy would perform his miracle were not able to blink; in fact, we had forgotten even how to breathe. It was hard to say what shocked us more: that the boy took those first steps towards us, or that on the sixth step his foot plunged into the water, followed by the rest of his body.

We stayed where we were, watching in silence. Perhaps we expected him to rise from the water on his own, but he didn't resurface. When the lifeguards dove into the lake, followed by the Reverend and half our congregation, it was too late—the boy had disappeared.

It is said that there are five stages of grief: denial, anger, bargaining, depression, acceptance. Perhaps there are even more. We all chose different stages to begin with.

Some of us believed a miracle *had* occurred. The boy *had* crossed the water on foot; he had simply not gone as far as we expected. And despite the dive teams—three days searching one small lake—his body was never found. He couldn't be dead. He was somewhere with his mother, who, like her son, had vanished without a trace.

These faithful believers went to the lake again on Sunday. The event had occurred on Good Friday, and this convinced them that, like Christ, the boy would rise again. They sat on the beach from sunrise to sunset, waiting for him to emerge from the water. Some claimed to have witnessed this resurrection, but offered no proof.

Others of us devised elaborate conspiracy theories. One of the more popular: that the council, in their greed for members and money, had built a ledge for the boy to walk on, yet he had lost his footing. That no such ledge was discovered seemed of little significance. Other theories explained the boy's escape: air tanks, underwater caves and tunnels, smoke-and-mirrors magic tricks.

As with all those who die before we are ready for them to leave us—Elvis, Lennon, Marilyn, Jesus himself—there were sightings of the boy: at McDonald's drive-thrus, in ferry lineups, on television newscasts from Afghanistan or Singapore, in shots of spectators at soccer matches and in game-show studio audiences.

We longed to believe; yet at the same time, most of us had started to feel ashamed of ever believing at all. What good had come of it? For the loss of the boy, we blamed Edith Stone. We blamed the council and the Reverend. We blamed each other and we blamed ourselves.

Eventually, almost all of us left Grace Lutheran; we turned to congregations across the city, or elsewhere on the religious spectrum—to temples and synagogues, circles of chanting strangers in the forest. We turned back to our runes and tarot cards, our Kabbalah studies, our drug-induced hallucinations. Or simply back to our disbelief.

Sarah Gillian

The Reverend made the Youth Group all split up to sell the T-shirts. I didn't feel like doing it. I just didn't. So I kept walking and walking until I could barely even see the crowd. Until all I could hear was this hum of noise. I went to this spot that my friends and I sometimes go to in the summer, the other side of the lake—across from the back of the island—and I sat down and just started throwing rocks into the water. I just thought it was so crazy, all the stuff about the boy being the next Jesus, or whatever. My parents and my friends, they talked as if it was a fact, and none of them had seen a single miracle.

I was watching the ripples the stones made when they skimmed the surface of the lake, and then I started feeling this thing in my head, this voice or something that was whispering, "What if it is real, what if he can do it?" And I raised my head, and I swear—I did see him. I saw him rise from the water until he was standing on the surface of the lake. He came towards me. I wasn't scared or shocked or anything; I just felt warm. He walked or glided or whatever until he was at the shore. He was so close, his legs brushed against my elbow. But I didn't say a thing. I don't know why, I just didn't. And neither did he. He smiled at me and kept walking, over the rock and into the trees. And I watched him. I watched until he disappeared.

ON CROWSNEST MOUNTAIN

AIR: THE MOLECULAR CHORUS

We are carbon dioxide, nitrogen, and oxygen. Argon. We are whispers of trace elements: elementary helium, iodine, krypton, neon. We are ozone. We are nitrogen dioxide, ammonia and xenon, methane and iodine, nitrous oxide. We are carbon monoxide.

We are carriers of waves. Of light and sound. We are harvesters harvesting: pollen, spores, sea spray, and smoke. Dust. And we are gatherers of vapour, skimming across water, gliding over grass. Creators of clouds.

We are still.

Or we are storming, with charged solar particles sent down to strike, flaring ribbons. Ripping night.

And we are surging through the veins of the living. Predator and prey, we are carried in their blood. We fill lungs. We are breath. Echoes we recall, always. A gauze of thoughts and memories.

On Crowsnest Mountain stand a man and a woman. Him breathing steadily, to still his speeding pulse. And her, fast and quick, she is gasping. She is summoning. So we hurl ourselves towards them, those mouths wide open. We go gusting, in.

Part I:

THE FATHER

There are some words it's best not to think about. Which is why I elect to think of only one: *rock*. Like the ones piled underfoot, a goddamn avalanche waiting to happen. Every lunge forward accompanied by a backwards roll, gravity directing its attention to my ass. Is this scree, then? And are we adding a dimension to the boy's epic adventure stories, experiencing it for ourselves? The boy and his stories. The boy. Like a fucking minefield, this train of thought.

Erica is oblivious to the inherent danger of the situation. The hazards involved. Middle-aged bodies tumbling and cracking open. Blind to the obvious, because she sees a point to us being here. A reason! As if reason is anything but a faulty construct. Reasoning. Reasonable. "It is reasonable to feel this way given the circumstances." From now on, reason will be banished to that writhing snakepit of things best left unspoken and unthought.

Replaced with this: *lichen*. Germanic-sounding, no? Spoken by a man in leather breeches pulling goats

towards the market. Lichen being the staple of a goat's
diet. Licked off rocks with its scrub brush of a tongue.
Mountain goats survive primarily, predominantly, on
papery plants. Recalling the source of this fact is a risk not
worth taking, so instead I will contemplate the amount
of lichen one goat must lick in a lifetime. And whether
lichen's hue is related to nutritional value. Or flavour. Is
it safe to assume that kids, like human children, consider
white more edible than green? And does the abundance
of orange lichen suggest it is consumed as a last resort?
And since when is lichen orange? Or black? Could it be
that lichen is the only existing black vegetation? Besides
the blackberry. Which might not be considered vegetation
to begin with, and for which *black* is a misnomer anyway,
the berry being as purple as Erica's tam.

The infamous tam-o'-shanter, most hideous of head
coverings. Do Scots even wear such things anymore, or
are tams for tourists only? This tam purchased by Erica in
the Glasgow airport a decade ago. Though the Glasgow
airport, and all memories related to the summer the boy
was twelve, will not be called up. Period. Whether or not
they are triggered by tam-wearing. A tam, if reflected
upon without sentimentality, is nothing more than a
Scottish beret. Authentic berets being just as obsolete
as authentic tam-o'-shanters, worn solely by the sort of
affected American expats who lug their easels daily to the
banks of the Seine.

I have just snorted aloud. Must have, because Erica
has turned to face me, blocking my ascent, and because

the low-level buzzing that has thus far accompanied the climb has ended. The buzzing in question being Erica herself. Or more precisely, her monologue about what we are looking for. About *whom* we are looking for.

I shake my head. "Go on."

And on she goes. And on and on. Not that I can decipher meaning. I have learned to block out the dangerous wound-ripping words of my wife.

Except. She's not moving, still facing me and trying to create that thing she always declared to the boy was all-important: eye contact. I am practically powerless against this. "Huh?" I say. And I really am listening now.

"You know what I'm thinking?" Erica asks.

Oh.

Yes, I could say, I know precisely. Excuse me as I plumb the depths of my subconscious. We'll haul everything up, then watch it expand to grotesque proportions, gather up noisemakers and form a parade.

"Do you know what *I'm* thinking?" I say instead. And Erica takes a deep breath as though she's been waiting for this all day. Like the students who come to review classes at the end of the semester, expecting I'll reveal the secrets of the final exam. But I'm not the kind of man to satisfy expectations. Erica, of all people, should know this.

"What?" she says quietly. Memories are standing on each other's shoulders, straining to break through to the surface.

"I'm thinking about this," I say, expanding my arms to encompass everything: the rock pile called mountain, the gathering clouds, Erica, myself. She's almost trembling now. Leaning forward so far she might tip over. "I'm thinking how useless it is to be here."

She just looks at me. Tenderly she looks, like the snake charmer that she is. The memories slip past their mesmerized captors. The loss of our son to weeks at summer camp, to trips to his grandparents, to the cluttered confines of the basement in his teenage years, to his parallel universe of priorities, to his friends, to a city that was too far away. What can I do to stop them? What can I say?

"You look ridiculous in that fucking hat," is what I come up with. And with this, she does turn from me. She starts climbing again.

"I'm finished," I say to her back. And I sit and stare at the ground beside me, trying to fill my head with only what is there. Rock, I whisper. Rock, rock, rock, like I'm meditating on the sound of it. Like a rock, rock hard, hard rock, rock on. Am I doing this correctly? Rock solid. Solid as rock. Don't rock the boat. Sinking like a stone. Stones in the pocket of goddamn Virginia Woolf. Enough! Rock. My Rock. Erica. Erica. Erica.

She's far ahead now, near the sheer limestone chimney. She shouldn't be alone up there. She shouldn't be here to begin with. It's not safe. It's not right. And it's not going to change anything. But try saying that to Erica. Same for him, try talking sense into that boy. Nothing doing. Can you ever rein in a person like that? Can you save them from themselves? You can't, is the answer. So don't even try.

Part II:

THE MOTHER

I'm finished, Sam says, and maybe he only means he's finished climbing, that he will go no farther, but it's also clear that he's finished playing along. He's not given up faith, just his show of faith. Real faith he didn't have to begin with.

But there are a host of reasons our son would abandon his tent, his car, a pot caked with macaroni and swarmed by flies. And why he would walk to Chinook Lake and throw his hiking boots into the water. And his pants. There are reasons why our son would turn from the lake then, and go elsewhere. Into the forest, or up a mountain. Away. Why he would not wade into the water until he was well beyond his depth, exhausted, his inhaler forgotten in his glovebox, this boy of ours who could barely swim.

That Nicola had just moved from their apartment was a devastation, but our son was not desolate. *To the Lighthouse*, pressed open on his sleeping bag, means nothing. An assigned text for school.

The discarded pants (is there anyone to identify that these were pants he was actually wearing?): Carhartts patched with duct tape and containing, in their pockets, not stones, but the Ford's key threaded onto a twist-tie. Also a water-wrecked photograph folded in half then half again, and two yellow guitar picks. Also a phone card imprinted with Nicola's name. Also his wallet. But this is not evidence enough. Sam may maintain that the only possibility is the one that is most *realistic*, but Sam is not a mother, and does not feel the heart of his child beating in his gut.

They've been searching since yesterday and haven't found a body in that lake.

I can feel Derek here.

Crowsnest was what he talked about the last time he called, from the pay phone in Blairmore City Campground—two hours on the highway was all it took for his great escape. He was camping, but promised he'd be back in Lethbridge when we arrived. This call made the day before we left Victoria with the intention of driving eight hundred kilometres to help him fill his empty apartment.

The first time he called to talk about Crowsnest, he was seventeen and I thought he had met a girl. His voice lilting on the telephone, those breathy pauses. Guess what I just did? he asked. And I was almost certain that I didn't want to know. This was after he spent his first summer away with his friend Carl. Roughing it for two months in the Kananaskis—herding kids up hills, onto horses, out of trouble. Driving home through Crowsnest Pass, the boys had been pulled from the highway and up the dirt road to the mountain's base, transfixed.

Derek didn't make it to the top that first time. The ascent started too late, the wind was high, the rock cairns blended with their surroundings so that they were almost imperceptible. The boys couldn't find the route, and so they tried to cross the scree to the other face. It wasn't until they were halfway that they understood the impossibility of that feat. And by that time, to quote our son, they were scared shitless.

When he told me all this, I thought about Sam. Or more precisely, I thought about going AWOL from a high school dance, then parking on the edge of town in that rusted pickup of his and expecting my father's face to appear, pressed to the glass, at any moment. I thought about how fear has a way of marking the beginning of a love affair.

Crowsnest was never a phase. Even Sam realized it, because he didn't tease the way he did about everything else. *How are those violin lessons?* When the instrument had for weeks served no more than a decorative purpose. *When are we going to have something to hang in the hall?* While fiddling with the still-sealed tubes of oil paint Derek requested for his birthday. Even when the spark was still alive, Sam didn't let up: *What?* Every dinnertime our son came to the table with microwaved slabs of nut loaf. *A vegetarian, still?*

But when Derek talked about the mountain, we both just listened. In that sense, we were a united front. We both, though hesitantly, supported the Lethbridge move, Derek going to school in Arthur Erickson's dungeon masterwork: a slab of cement dug into a coulee. And all, it seemed, so he could be closer to Crowsnest. *Romantic*, Sam snorted, though only to me. *He can drive there at night so its face is the first thing he sees when the sun rises.*

We did that ourselves. Drove yesterday from Creston to Chinook Lake, and then slept in the car at the base. To be closer, I said. Maybe Sam agreed because he thought I meant closer to the searchers.

Now, there sits Sam against a boulder, his arms crossed tight over his chest. The backdrop like one of Derek's photographs: the Seven Sisters in a row, a wash of greens and greys. Some things need to be seen to be proved real. And other things are even more unbelievable close up than the story of them ever can be. Like this mountain, and that our son climbed to the top. How many times?

I understand the draw. Everything is sharper up here. The smell is like scorched dust lodged in my throat, and the clouds throw jagged shadows that ripple towards me over the rocks, then bite the warmth from my skin. My pulse throbs wildly. But I won't be deterred. Because if I reach the top, I'll find Derek alive.

The day before we slept at the trailhead parking lot, we slept in Creston Valley Motel. This was after some fellow campers found Derek's clothes. I lay on the floral bedspread watching Olympic highlights, and Sam sat beside me, alternately holding his head in his hands and staring at the side of my face. My body was aching from a day in the passenger seat, the air conditioner broken just outside Osoyoos and

Sam fiddling with the knob, refusing to open the windows as the desert sun beat through the glass. Not an actual desert, he had said as the licorice at my feet melted, as my skin baked, as my temper flared. After the police called, he had given up and opened the windows wide.

Halfway through a Michael Phelps montage, Sam switched off the set. "What do we do next?"

"Find Derek." It was that simple.

"Erica!" he said—he shouted. And then he started to cry.

For a while I tried to come up with something to say, but there was nothing. I closed my eyes. I fell asleep. And when I woke, it was to Derek. The smell of him at least: warm and thick, like damp wool. A sign we were close.

The bedside phone was on the floor, its cord stretched into the bathroom. "Denial," I heard Sam say. "How long do I let this last?"

But the next morning, when I told him I wanted to climb Crowsnest, that I wanted us to search for Derek ourselves, he only pressed his fingertips against his eyelids for a moment.

Derek is on the mountaintop; in my mind, I see him clearly. There's his hiking hat—that pilled orange toque with the pompom on top. Also the Scarpa boots, with the bells I made him tie to his laces to scare off wildlife.

But the Scarpas were found in the lake.

Because Derek had taken them off, wanting to let his

feet breathe. He's in his sneakers, his camera swung over his shoulder on that threadbare Guatemalan cord.

Except that the camera was in the tent, beneath his pillow, the searchers said. And the toque too. The filthy hat that I threatened for years to make disappear, I had buried my face in yesterday, inhaling the scent of my son.

And so I have to disassemble that picture, to pull away the pieces that don't fit. When I see what little I'm left with, I ask myself: is this really what I believe?

Yes! I respond, aloud, at once. *No* comes the echo from deep within me, from the part that is collapsing. Why would Derek's clothes be in Chinook Lake if he didn't go in there himself? And why would Derek go into the water when he can't swim? Is it possible that Derek is where everyone believes he is: tangled in the weeds at the bottom of that lake?

I shut my mind to the answer, keep climbing to the place that holds on to my son. But here, at the base of the towering chimney, the rocks are too steep to climb on their own and the chain fixed to them is slack. The missing bolt becomes apparent when my foot slips from its hold. And then I'm sliding down scree, slamming to a stop against a large rock. This pain I feel isn't from the fall, it's from the picture expanding to fill my head. It's from the realization that Derek is never coming home. And the possibility that he wanted it that way.

And there is nothing I can do about it. Nothing for me to do at all except to lie here, until I am desiccated by the sun, turned papery as lichen. Until I am caught by a gust of wind and blown away. Until I see it, standing at the top of the chimney like an apparition. A young, lone goat.

Part III:
THE WITNESS

Grazing on the ridge, I watch the climbers.

Careful, Mother says. Be the rocks, be the air, be not there.

Afraid of humans? the old ones say, as I duck away.

They do not hide, so why should I?

Humans are dangerous, Mother says. They carry sticks that call to death. Shoot fire.

And the old ones agree. *Be fearful of humans, but not of these two. Come out from your hiding place. Look.*

But Mother says no. Who can be sure a human is safe?

The old ones can. The old ones know.

Go, says Mother. Go away.

The old ones tell Mother these humans are lost.

But Mother says no. They are going the way the others go. Up.

Yes, up, the old ones laugh. *To the top to see the view. But that's not all they're looking for.*

No? I ask.

Away, Mother tells me. Go away.

She stays on the ridge to watch the man below. And I watch the woman, who climbs on alone. Streams of scree slide with her every step, in rivulets.

Rocks can become rivers, the old ones say, *a crest of rubble rushing. A crust of rubble covering. Everything. And silence folding into it all that crashes and collapses. A cloud of dust obscuring any light that endures. The sunrise grey as dusk as the humans went on dreaming. An endless dream in an endless night under Turtle Mountain. In the town of Frank.*

On that mountain that gave way, the old ones say, *our relatives were grazing and gazing at the sky. They were caught in the current. They were carried with the river. Collapsing. And crashing. Everywhere.*

This happened long ago. But the old ones hold the story in their bodies. They have breathed it.

How?

Not fleet-footed as you, child. But we are wiser.

They speak to the dead, Mother says, and the old ones concur.

To ghosts.

Ghosts of whom?

Not whom, but what, the old ones laugh.

What, then?

Everything. Everything breathing and everything not. Every place. Every happening and happened. We find their traces in the air. It's all still there.

Mother hasn't seen these ghosts, but she believes: the old know everything.

But I know things too.

Things that gather like storm clouds in my head. A

word: *dead*. And the face of a man I've seen before. What does this mean? Then more: a grizzly and her cub on the shore of Chinook Lake. And him caught between them, plunging in to escape, kicking boots, shucking pants in his wake. Fear. As the sun sets, and the bears pace. And he tires of treading water.

And then a floating fullness takes its place. I clutch it close. But the old ones interrupt.

In a procession, they arrive at my side. *Do you know why the woman is here?* they ask.

Her son, I say.

And how can you tell?

I know. Everything flaps loosely, unfurled in the air.

Fleet-footed and wise, they say, *can it be so?*

I need to see her closer up.

Yes, child. Go.

When I climb, I collect. I take what is waiting, hanging there ripe and ready to pluck. I spin a story out of sky. I hold it tight. Is this right?

When I reach the chimney, she's there below. Look up, I demand. A silent call, but still she stands. Her eyes find mine. What do I do?

Hello, she says, then looks away.

No! Stay!

But what comes next? I've forgot.

I climb down towards her, and when I'm close, I see it on her face. Part of the story; all she knows. Oh.

Listen, I say, a mute command. Is there a way to show the rest? The story sits frozen, curled on my tongue. I take a breath.

The air floods out fast, thick with the soaring fullness of a son. A man. The woman gasps, deep and low. But how can I tell if she sees what I know?

Epilogue:

AIR: THE MOLECULAR CHORUS

When the woman parts her lips, we rush through mouth to trachea, to bronchi, bronchioles, alveoli, lungs. And we are held there.

Oxygen diffuses into blood, and with it comes a story. For we are carriers: of the keening of a grizzly cub, its mother on her haunches. Growling. Charging. And a boy treading water who cannot see the shore. Who can stay afloat no longer.

There's a beat without breath as everything's absorbed, and then we're exhaled. With a wail, we're sent outwards, rushing free. And we're whirling, spinning, turning, we are forcing, gusting, pressing, pushing past: a silent hoofed messenger, his herd still and watching. Pushing past: a man who is standing, to climb towards his wife. Pushing past: a small group of searchers who have gathered on a lakeshore. They have gathered by a body of a boy. But what they've found is no more than a vessel, empty. His spirit isn't lost, but flows everywhere, just like us. Is part of everything, just like us. He's joined our chorus of the infinite.

⚔ WINCHESTER .30-.30

Based on the events leading to the first trial
of Inuit men by the Canadian legal system.

AUGUST 1917

The gun was left untouched for most of the trial.
Untouched by the Spectators: the Oblate priests, hands
like folded paper on their black cassocks, and the others—
men and women with fingers white as caribou bones.
Untouched by the gavel-fisted Judge. Untouched even by
Sinnisiak, whose callused hands that tasted of blood and
ice caught nothing but yawns.

Only the Lawyer held her. He spoke to the Jury about
bullets found beside the Coppermine River while the pad
of his pointer finger skimmed her barrel and the cuff of his
silk gown blanketed her sight. And then he gripped her
shaft. There was relief in this attention, but it was dimin-
ished by the objects in his other hand: those three spent
cartridges. The gun had been barren for so long. It was
months ago that the Inspector, the man called LaNauze,
had wrapped her in deerskin and cast her aside. When he

did so, he had been imagining this room, this moment. But what did her future hold beyond it?

Sinnisiak and Uluksuk sat corralled in the prisoners' box, their bare feet plunged into buckets of ice water—a remedy against the Edmonton heat. Uluksuk flexed his fingers in his lap, and each time he did, the gun envisioned one of them curled around her trigger. He had held her only once, months ago, and never fired her. Then, she had closed herself to the taste of him, but she imagined it now: snow and lamp oil. Earth. His hands were not unlike Kormik's, the Trouble Maker, the man who had once claimed her. Not unlike the Hunter's, the man she longed for. But those hands were the only part of him that was familiar. In every other way he and Sinnisiak had transformed: their caribou skins were exchanged for prison-issue denims and their long hair was shorn off. Their bodies were wilted, and waiting.

Waiting for this: the verdict, spoken by the Judge and Jury. The Translator, Ilivanik, tugged the collar of his shirt, pulling the starched fabric away from his neck. His fingers tapped the rhythm of the Judge's speech, and then his lips formed words that sealed the men's fate: guilty, for the murder of two white men, two priests.

On the evidence table, the gun lay with the breviaries and surplice, with a bloodstained cassock, a human jaw-bone, and a yellowed diary—tilted suggestively towards the jury. All of these things were reminders of the Father—the gun's first owner—and of what she had done to him. But had she not already been absolved? Uluksuk and Sinnisiak were now being led away, their hands cuffed behind their backs. What she needed was another man to claim her.

And then the Inspector came. He left his seat in the courtroom and lingered beside her. As he ran his thumb over the cracks in her walnut stock, over the thinning blue of her barrel and magazine tube, over the checkered border of her hammer, over her lever, worn silver, she was certain he would take her into his arms. And he did. He lifted her and looked: through her sights, the semi-buckhorn rear and the front with its ivory bead. The Father had removed some of the pinch on the base around the blade for a better sight plane, and the Inspector's eyes rested there for a moment, then closed.

Pressed to his shoulder, the gun could see the future the Inspector was imagining: Sinnisiak and Uluksuk in the jailhouse in Fort Resolution, serving as guides for their captors until they could be cast aside, released northwards to the land of their beginnings. Until they could be released with guns of their own, and diseases to turn their lungs to lace and steal their breath, diseases not even the Shaman would be able to cure.

The Inspector saw all this, and then he opened his eyes. And though she tried to hold him, though she tried to use that force she had discovered long ago, she could not. He placed her on the table and turned away.

MAY 1916

The Hunter's hands were like caribou: strong and solid, but quiet in their approach. He did not often fire the gun, but when he did, there was always blood. An animal cracked open and leaking towards her; a taste of kill.

The Hunter had other weapons: knives, and a harpoon that had been his father's. Its tail of rope had carved thick scars into his palm, had claimed the tip of his finger, sawed it off as he hauled a seal above the ice hand over hand. The Hunter was never without the reminder of the harpoon on his flesh, but he was never without the gun either. He even lashed her to his back during seal hunts as he joined the procession of men crawling on their knees across the ice. Wrists black with frostbite, he would kneel beside a breathing hole with the harpoon in his hand and the gun nested between his legs.

The first winter that the gun lived with the Hunter, the caribou went south before the ice was thick. *What is the use of a gun*, the Hunter's wife said, *when there are no animals to shoot?* They shared the last of their dried fish with their neighbours, who were hungry also. Soon there was nothing. The Hunter's wife chewed on a sealskin boot. During this time, the Hunter left his tent each day and walked to the edge of the ice. And though, with bitter fingers, his wife pointed to the rust on the gun's barrel and the cracks in her shaft, every time the Hunter left the tent, it was the gun he carried with him. It was her he took comfort in.

The gun had become the Hunter's before the ice froze, and she remained his when it thawed, then froze, and thawed again. And not once did she long for the Shaman, the one called Illuga, the one who abandoned her well before he gave her up. In fact, she thought little of the Shaman and of the time before. The kills she made for the Hunter were atonements; with him she created a new and blameless history. And then one day she heard the Shaman's dogs in the distance. The Hunter and his wife left the tent as the sled approached.

The Shaman was watching her. Even from a distance, before he called out a greeting, she could tell. And the others watched her also: the group of white men, the Translator, whose tongue straddled two worlds, and Sinnisiak, who followed behind the rest. Sinnisiak, the trigger of her memories, the hands the gun knew well. The Hunter walked to meet them, and still the Hunter held her in his arms. Did he not realize that this other man was coming to reclaim her?

Once, the gun had been powerful. She had pulled men towards her. And now she tried to conjure this strength again, to use it to push the Shaman away. But it had been so long since she had discovered this force inside her, and equally long since she had striven to erase it. She had grown weak. She could do nothing to stop him.

"This is the gun of the Father," the Shaman said to the Translator, after the Hunter had shown the group into his tent. The Shaman pointed at her, cradled in the Hunter's lap. His finger was blunt, stiff as bone. "The weapon was traded." The Shaman did not say that it was he who had traded the gun to the Hunter, nor did the Hunter remind him, but he tightened his grip on her stock.

"This is the gun," the Translator repeated in the language of the white men, and then to the Hunter he said: "These white men will give you bullets and a shotgun, and you will give them this weapon."

"Yes," the Shaman said. He crossed the tent and placed his hands upon her. They were cold, just as the gun remembered them. And smooth, like the stones the river washed a dull, flat grey. The Hunter's fingers loosened. The Shaman pulled. The gun's last taste of the Hunter: his splayed fingers feathering her stock.

The white man called Inspector seized the gun without removing his deerskin mittens. She was not even given a final moment with the man who had redeemed her, so eager was he to carry her away. He took her from the tent and walked with her across the hard wavelets of ice. Despite the sun, which flared in the snow before him, he did not slow on his way to the harbour.

SEPTEMBER 1914

Besides the gun, the Shaman owned many things that had belonged to the Father, the gun's first owner — a Roman breviary, illustrated scripture-lesson books, pages of the priest's own words — things that were lashed to the Father's sled the day he died. To the Shaman, she was no

more important than these other, useless things. She was
not his only gun; he had shotguns and rifles both, given
to him by men at the Canadian Arctic Expedition Camp
at Bernard Harbour. And though she longed to redeem
herself, to make a kill to ward off hunger, to ward off fear,
the Shaman was fed by others—he was not hungry. And
he was afraid of nothing.

The guns were of little use to the Shaman, and little
value. His great treasure was the large silver crucifix the
Father had once worn around his neck. A thing with
no purpose. A thing that could do nothing for him. Yet,
whenever a visitor came to the Shaman's tent, he would
first offer a piece of frozen fish. And then he would boil
water over his seal-oil lamp, for tea that he served in cups
that bloomed pink with flowers. He would set these cups
onto saucers, and then he would take the first sip, pinch-
ing a thin handle between thumb and forefinger, and lifting the cup to his lips. After this display, he would draw
back the fur on his sleeping platform and produce from
beneath it the silver crucifix. This he would hang from
the centre of his tent by its silken cord, making sure it
was straight—the ebony rosary draped on one arm, the
alabaster one hanging from the other, prodded and pulled
until a perfect balance was achieved. Only when his guest
was suitably impressed would the Shaman allow him a
chance to speak.

Yes, the Shaman treasured the crucifix, but there was
something he desired more, something the gun had seen
in his dreams: a magic machine that turned small things

large and brought far things close. A machine owned by the Hunter. And this was why the Shaman invited the Hunter to his tent and greeted him wearing the Father's black cassock, which reached almost to his ankles. He also wore a small silver cross, which the Father had given him when he was alive. *So that when you die, you will go to the land above the sky.*

The gun had been with the Father when he said this, and she had seen his visions: a scene like the coloured illustration of Heaven that later the Shaman hung above his sleeping platform — brilliant, aching heat. The Shaman did not speak the Father's language, but he had touched his thumb and first two fingers to his forehead, then to the centre of his chest, and then left towards his heart and right again, the same way that the Father had done.

When the Hunter came, the Shaman placed the picture of Heaven on his sleeping platform, along with some of the Father's books. He poured tea and hung the crucifix. And then, from his display of guns, he chose her. He placed her in the Hunter's hands. The Hunter's palms were tundra, their scars and calluses like the jagged crests of windblown snow.

"This is a good gun," the Shaman said, though he had shot her only twice. When he first held the gun, his icy fingers had found the rust on her barrel and the small crack in her shaft, but the Hunter's hands didn't dwell on these places. He ran his thumb the entire length of her.

"Yes," the Hunter said. "This is a very good gun."

Outside the tent, the Hunter set up his telescope —

tilting it towards the place called Heaven. Above, luminous clouds spiralled outwards like frayed rope. When the Hunter departed, he left the telescope behind and carried her with him.

OCTOBER 1913

It was Uluksuk who held her when the men returned to Coronation Gulf. His hands were stained with blood. She had longed for these hands, but now she closed herself to the taste of them. She was quavering. Maybe this was because of the tremor through Uluksuk's body, but more likely it was because of what she had done.

Better to be held by Uluksuk than the other, Sinnisiak. The one who had caressed her afterwards, who had polished her shame until she throbbed from it. Sinnisiak who had set her on the snow to retrieve a knife, who had taken the knife to the Father's body as the priest's final dreams seeped into the snow.

Did these men own her now? Would every kill become a reminder of this first one they shared? The gun thought of the Trouble Maker. At night, his hands would grasp his wife, cupping her softness, stroking her warmth. Oil and animal flesh, his fingers were greedy with desire, but tender in their advances. He had held the gun in much the same way. Perhaps Uluksuk and Sinnisiak knew of the Trouble Maker's claim on her. Perhaps it was to him she was being taken.

But when they reached the edge of the frozen ocean, it was the Shaman's snow house they entered. Inside, the sleeping platform was piled thick with furs. The Shaman's three wives sat, stitching sealskins. Above them, the Shaman stood, fingers twisting the small silver cross that hung against his collarbone, the Father's gifted salvation. And across the snow house, in front of the row of rifles the Shaman owned, crouched the Trouble Maker.

Sinnisiak did not wait for the Shaman to ask him to speak. "We saw the white men," he said.

The Trouble Maker clenched his fists. "Are they far away?"

"They are dead," Sinnisiak said. "We had to kill them." He turned to Uluksuk, motioning for him to show her to the others, to display her guilt, but Uluksuk was staring at the doorway, moaning.

"Uluksuk thinks their shadows followed us," Sinnisiak said. "But we sliced open their bodies and ate pieces of their livers."

"Good," said the Shaman. "That is the right way."

"Uluksuk says white men are like spirits," Sinnisiak said. "Because they live far away and speak with a different tongue."

"Yes," said the Shaman. His fingers lifted from his necklace and motioned for Uluksuk, pulling him closer. "And like spirits, the white men brought trouble with them. They are the reason the ice is thin, and the caribou have left, and the children are hungry."

The others turned towards Uluksuk, who was still

trying to ward off the priests' ghosts with his song of fear. As the Father had, Uluksuk held dreams in his head: four pillars holding up the sky, framing the world he knew, and beyond them a place of riotous colour like in the Father's pictures. White men with weapons crawled from their world into the next.

"Maybe when they return, they will be angry," Sinnisiak said, breathing aloud Uluksuk's visions, "and things will be worse."

The Shaman stepped away from the others. A yelp raced through his throat as his familiar—the dog he housed inside his body—released itself into the air. Uluksuk's fingers relaxed around her as the Shaman collapsed, quivering, onto the floor and his familiar ripped towards the shadows, growling and chasing them away. The Shaman's hands were taut, his fingers fierce.

When the familiar slipped back inside the Shaman and silence swallowed the last of its barks, Uluksuk placed the gun beside the Shaman's heaving body. Though the Trouble Maker's hands hungered for the gun, though his touch alone would have redeemed her, she was left on the ground. Nothing that was given to the Shaman was ever taken away.

OCTOBER 1913

The gun was wrapped in Father Rouvière's wool blanket, tucked between the priest's sleeping body and the snow-house wall. She was steeped in cold—not from the ice she was pressed against but from the priest's night visions, curling tightly around her: a giant ship anchoring at the mouth of the Coppermine, the hold filled with lumber to build a church for Eskimos. Eskimo baptisms, Eskimo marriages, Eskimo last rites. Always the same desolate dreams, when the Father was awake and sleeping both. Though Le Roux, the Young Priest, clenched his rifle in his fist as he slept, though he carried this weapon into his unconscious, when the Father slept, the gun was abandoned. His dream hands held Bibles and Eskimo children; they never held her.

The gun longed for heat. She longed for the man across the snow house, the Trouble Maker. Tasting of oil and animal flesh, his hands had touched her only once, but they had been ravenous. In his sleep story, she saw the day two summers earlier when the Father had offered her up in exchange for him spending a winter in the priests' cabin. He had refused then, had not wanted to stay at Lake Imaernik, a place far from the seals and his family. He had left for the coast. But he had come back, and had taken the priests to winter with him beside the frozen ocean. Now, in his dream, he grasped the gun with thick fists. He pulled her from the Father's hands. He wanted what she wanted: the crack of gunpowder, the snow stained with blood. His side of the bargain made at Lake Imaernik had been fulfilled; she belonged to him. And yet his waking fingers had never touched her.

Aside from the Father, only the Trouble Maker's wife

held her. When the woman sifted through the priests' piles of fur and fabric for holes to stitch closed, her hands glanced the gun's stock and lingered on her trigger. The fury that leaked to the surface of her body, that stained her fingers, was over a gun horded by a man who could shoot nothing, who fed her with bullets that only sank into the canvas of snow. The Trouble Maker's wife saw the Father the same way the gun herself did: as a man capable of only unimportant things—singing and teaching others to touch their heads and chests. And she was trapped by the Father also: just as the gun could not escape the Father's possession, the Trouble Maker's wife could not escape her obligation to the white priests. She had no choice but to help these men who travelled without women of their own. She had no choice but to feed them, though there weren't enough fish to feed the dogs. Sometimes in her rage she would take things from the priests—things like sugar and tea—payment for the work she did with her needle and the food she shared. But she always returned the gun to the pile of wealth the Father stacked upon the floor.

Night stories swirled around the snow house. The Trouble Maker dreamt the gun, his wife dreamt the dogs—howling with hunger. But still the Father's visions were holy water and hymns. Even the Young Priest called these things impossible. He told the Father that Eskimos could not be taught. That people on a frozen tundra could know nothing of daily bread, sheep, and shepherds. That Eskimos could never comprehend Jesus, nailed to a cross for their sins, when their only wood was driftwood, all of it small and too precious to use. But still Father Rouvière dreamt. He dreamt of God as a boat maker and sheep as caribou. He dreamt of Eskimo fishermen, their catches multiplying. The gun tried to drag him from these thoughts, to pull his hands towards her, but she always failed. As the sun sank towards the horizon, the Father became blind to anything but his dreams.

When they had reached Coronation Gulf, the Young Priest turned in all directions: behind them, where there was an endless roll of treeless hills, to the left and right, where a gravel beach extended for hundreds of miles, in front to the sheet of ice that covered the Gulf. The sun was low.

"This is like a photograph," the Young Priest had said.

"Yes," said Father Rouvière. His visions had started; in them, the land was biblical, a desert without heat.

"An overexposed photograph," said the Young Priest.

Father Rouvière didn't answer. He was envisioning a Moses of the Eskimos forging a path to salvation.

"In a month the sun will go down, and it won't come up until January." The wind was damp and strong, and the Young Priest turned his back to it and to the Father. Wrapped in blankets on the sled, the gun felt for the first time the bitterness of solitude.

Now, as the Father dreamt ships of lumber and Eskimo weddings, a hand slipped through the folds of the wool blanket. Rouvière's hands were thin, his fingers delicate. They tasted of smoke and of his devotion to the books he was never without. These hands were leather and grease, rough and tremendous.

"This is ours," the Trouble Maker told his wife as he placed the gun at the opposite end of the snow house, a sealskin covering the length of her stock and most of her shaft. The two Eskimos left, and the gun waited. She waited for the thick cord of Father Rouvière's dreams to unravel, for the hymns to fade and with them the upturned faces of the Father's night worshippers. When they did, when the Father finally opened his eyes to the day without light, it was her that his hands sought first. They groped for her in the blanket she had been wrapped in, fingers fumbling the empty folds of cloth. And then he threw himself onto his knees, the blanket unfurling as he felt the ground for her body.

"Le Roux," Rouvière shouted. "Who has my gun?"

His rifle still clenched in his cold fist, the Young Priest placed a finger on the trigger. "Only Kormik could have taken the gun, and now we will take it back." He stood and pulled his parka over his cassock.

The Young Priest left the snow house with his rifle drawn, and Rouvière followed at his heels, polishing his rosary, repeating a three-word prayer of *mistake, misplaced, misunderstanding.* The gun waited for the sealskin to be pulled off her. Who would take her into his hands next—the Father, his eyes now opened to her worth, or the Trouble Maker, his fingers pulsing with heat?

Despite her hopes, it was the flat taste of woman that retrieved her. The Trouble Maker's mother marched into the snow house and lifted her from her hiding place. Her hands were carved with scars and age, but they were reticent. Her fingertips flavourless. Once outside, she walked past her son, his body stayed by two men, Sinnisiak and Uluksuk. Past the Old Man, Koeha, from the neighbouring snow house — his dark eyes fixed to the priests. When she reached the Father, she held the gun towards him. He gripped her stock loosely with a mittened hand, then buried her in his parka. He did not caress her. And then the Old Man put his palm on Rouvière's shoulder and turned the Father towards the Trouble Maker's snow house. The priests pulled their sled to the doorway and the Old Man stood guard as they piled it with all they owned. She was lashed to the top, forsaken.

Because the priests' pair of dogs were weak and thin as skeletons, the Old Man gave them two more. He also gave them directions, his silent fingers pointing away from the coast. And when the priests began to walk, he walked beside them, until only the tops of the snow houses were visible. Then he turned around.

Rouvière drove the sled, and Le Roux ran ahead with the dogs. The gun's stock was crusted in ice.

"There will be game past the treeline," Rouvière told the other, but he was seeing visions still: shapes in the horizon that were either trees or devils.

The snow was soft, and it swallowed the men's legs with every step. It took three days for the priests to walk ten miles. Three days without food or shelter. Three days of the gun atop the sled, untouched.

And then, when the priests were talking about last rites, and whether it was time to perform them on each other, when the gun had resolved herself to a forever-barren chamber, to her walnut stock rotting with the snowmelt in the spring, Sinnisiak and Uluksuk arrived. They had no sled of their own.

"They will steal from us," the Young Priest said, and he pulled the gun from the sled and handed her to the Father. "They have come to take all we have."

But Sinnisiak and Uluksuk said they were going else-where, to visit family far away. The gun watched their hands, pointing into darkness. She had not tasted these fingers, but she longed to. She knew both Sinnisiak and Uluksuk would use her in a way Father Rouvière never could: each bullet that entered her chamber striking its target and drawing blood. She wanted the men to stay.

And so did the Father. He asked the Eskimos to har-ness themselves beside the dogs and pull the sled south-wards. And because he promised traps in exchange for this service, the men agreed. For a day they pulled, and at night they built a snow house and lined it with caribou skins.

That night, the Eskimos dreamt of women with dark eyes and warm bodies, great feasts of female flesh. But the Father's mind was as dark as the air that pressed against his open eyes. And though his gloved hands clutched her, she was alone.

Morning brought a blizzard and Uluksuk and Sinnisiak refused to go farther south. They departed northwards into the blowing snow, towards the camp they had set off to visit the day before. Their departure sealed her fate: she would belong to the Father forever. She would be lashed to sleds or wrapped in blankets instead of gripped by bare and hungry hands.

The gun longed for Sinnisiak and Uluksuk to return and carry her away. Her desire spilled from her, lifting with the wind, whipping through the blowing snow. And like a magnet against a compass needle, it pulled the men back. She had not known such things were possible, but she could feel them drawing nearer. Soon they were there at the edge of the Coppermine River, where the Young Priest had stood only moments before. Where he had left a cache of bullets to lighten the weight of his load.

"How did the white men arrive here before us, when they are travelling in a different direction?" Uluksuk whispered to Sinnisiak.

"The white men have magic powers," Sinnisiak said. But it was she who was powerful. She who had turned these men around without them noticing. If they had looked up, they would have seen the sled behind the next snowbank, seen that she was almost close enough to touch. But they did not look. Not until Le Roux had spotted them himself and pushed through the snow to the place where they stood.

Violently, the Young Priest waved the men away from the bullets with the handle of his axe. And then, with its

blade pointed towards them, he shook the harnesses on
the sled.

"If they want what's ours, they'll earn it," he said to
Father Rouvière. The Father said nothing; the shadows in
his mind had grown as vast as the surrounding darkness.
There were caribou bones in the snow beside him, bones
piled like driftwood, but he didn't seem to notice. He had
not eaten for a very long time.

Sinnisiak and Uluksuk put on the harnesses, but
Uluksuk cried that he would not go to white man's country. The Young Priest shouted for silence, but Uluksuk
only howled, his wail like that of a dying animal. It was
then that the Young Priest hit Uluksuk with his fists. And
again with the axe handle, and with the strap he used on
the dogs. Uluksuk turned towards Rouvière, the Father
who always softened the edges of the other, but he was
faced away.

"Will we die in their country?" Uluksuk demanded
of Sinnisiak.

Sinnisiak didn't have an answer, but in his boot he had
a knife. While Le Roux whipped Uluksuk's arms with his
strap, Sinnisiak drove the blade into the Young Priest's
back. Le Roux screamed his agony, loud enough to drag
Father Rouvière back into the world of ice and wind. Loud
enough to make the Father reach for her. But Sinnisiak's
hands were faster, and he grasped her stock and pulled
her away. Sinnisiak held her tight against his shoulder, his
cheek pressed to her sight. His embrace so enveloped her
that she felt only the rivers of warmth coursing beneath

his skin. She did not parse his subtleties of touch until after his finger curved around her trigger. Until he fired her three times, three bullets carving three paths into frozen mist.

When she looked through those tunnels in the sky, she expected to see her future unfurling in front of her. But all that was there was the Father, falling. As the final bullet found its mark, all she saw was the red shame of her desire in the spreading stain of blood.

⚞ THE WINDSPIR SISTERS' HOME FOR THE DYING

THE BIRTH OF THE WINDSPIR SISTERS

At first, the people of Remming trumpeted the birth of six Windspir sisters, but Violet lived for three days only. They celebrated five, but by week's end Henrietta was also gone. But even a Windspir Quartet was reason for rejoicing. Especially considering the size of the girls, huddled in their single hospital isolette like a clutch of nestlings. And to the nurses, the girls did seem like birds — newly hatched, found fallen. They heated them with lamps, fed them droplet by droplet through syringes, and finally, once their gentle coos had turned to screeches and soft down began to grow on their scalps, they executed their release.

Four daughters is a blessing, the nurses assured Mr. Douglas Windspir, the day he took his daughters home. His neighbours tried to remind themselves of this also, so that they would be convinced, so that when they arrived on the Windspir doorstep with crocheted blankets and casseroles, their faces wouldn't arrange themselves into masks of pity. But this was hard. Because what Mr. Windspir had gained—four children, four new mouths to feed—seemed unlikely to make up for his losses: two infants buried before baptism, a wife dead from childbirth.

Time muffles loss, each day adding a layer of distance between a person and the pains they've suffered, the pains they've witnessed. After a while, the people of Remming spoke of the four Windspir sisters as though four was the number they had always been. Mr. Windspir did the same. So worn from giving when so much had already been taken from him, he couldn't be blamed for concerning himself with only the solid things, his living children: Isabelle, Sarah, Elizabeth, and Maude. But even as infants, the girls were keenly aware of their spirit sisters curled beside them in their bassinets. The Windspir sisters always knew that they were six. Violet and Henrietta, though prone to sudden disappearances, though adept at passing through furniture, were just as real to the living Windspirs as each other.

THE SPIRIT SISTERS

All six sisters grew together in the cramped quarters of the Windspir homestead: the post-and-beam farmhouse at the front of the property; Mr. Windspir's vegetable garden to the left of it—the pole beans, the runner beans, the broad beans, the bush beans, the occasional misshapen zucchini; to the right, the mossy earth with the small copse of oak and spruce, which the sisters referred to as the woods; and in back, the rutted, overgrown field. The property was surrounded by the thick wooden stakes and rusted wire of an ageing pasture fence.

In the real world, the small town of Remming was beyond that fence, but in the spirit world, it was as though the Windspir property was afloat in an endless, pulsing White. The White was warm, though Violet and Henrietta didn't know to describe it as such. The spirit sisters never ventured to the edges of the homestead; the pull was magnetic, and they were afraid of being torn away.

To Violet and Henrietta, the Windspir homestead was the one solid thing, and the living Windspirs were the shadows that crossed through it. Though whereas their sisters were only muted, somewhat blurred, their father was faded almost to invisible. They saw him only through the items in his possession, through their sisters' stories.

To the living sisters, the lost Windspirs were their pale twins; they were a secret shared between them. The spirit sisters were only ever present to their siblings, and while the living Windspir sisters savoured secrets, this one had its limitations. For instance, on occasion Violet and Henrietta wreaked havoc on the homestead. They were confined to the Windspir property even when their living sisters were elsewhere, and, like all children, when left to their own devices, they grew restless. There were things broken or misplaced, walls drawn on, teddy bears dug hollow. A precious porcelain doll once belonging to Mrs. Windspir had its face smashed beyond repair.

Many children have imaginary friends on whom they blame their misdeeds, but few invoke as excuses their long-dead siblings. Even to a man like Mr. Windspir—who never made it farther than the coffee pot on Sunday mornings—this seemed a particularly unchristian offence. The living sisters were punished for their sisters' crimes, and punished further for not admitting to them.

Eventually, the living Windspirs realized it was best simply to apologize for Violet and Henrietta's misbehaviour, and stopped greeting their father's reprimands with wilfulness and indignation. Instead, they were chastened. They displayed suitable remorse. Not long afterwards, Violet and Henrietta tired of their transgressions.

THE WINDSPIR SISTERS GROW UP

Once the living Windspirs passed through their teenage years, they became nurses at the Remming Hospital. Their shifts were handed out in parcels, and between them the sisters decided who would work when, who would do what. Their lives changed, but not in every way. There were no apartments in town, as there were for the other young ladies of Remming. And though there were suitors, there were none who lasted, none whose promises appealed. For the living sisters, the idea of leaving the Windspir homestead was unfathomable. Only in their childhood home and the surrounding property did their lost sisters exist for them. How could they trade this for homes, cities, lives that were empty?

Maybe there were people in Remming who found it strange, the four Windspir sisters living with their father well into their twenties, sharing their one small room in the Windspir house even as the space they took up increased. But no one said a thing. The Windspirs lived like that, Mr. Windspir in one room, his daughters in the other, the kitchen between, until just after the sisters turned thirty, and Mr. Windspir died.

THE DEATH OF MR. WINDSPIR

It was Mr. Windspir's heart that failed him, and considering the pain inflicted on that particular organ over his lifetime, this was not surprising.

It was not a sudden thing, but it had a sudden start. One moment, Henrietta and Violet were watching the quivering eyelids of their sleeping sisters, prying into their dreams. The next moment, their father was beside them.

Mr. Windspir took one look at Violet and Henrietta, these mirrors of his living daughters, and knew them instantly. They were glimmers, wisps—halfway there and halfway not. Still, it was enough. It was more than he had ever hoped for.

"Am I dead, then?" he asked. Henrietta and Violet were unsure. They had never met a dead person.

But Mr. Windspir was not dead. When a person slips in and out of consciousness, it is not like slipping in and out of sleep, but like slipping in and out of worlds. And in the days that followed, Mr. Windspir's time was divided between the world of his living daughters and the world of the spirit ones. In both worlds he was taken care of; in both worlds he was loved.

"Who expected," Mr. Windspir remarked often in the month of his dying, "that the end would be such an outstanding experience? That I would meet my lost children?" Though the pain was extreme, death, for Mr. Windspir, was a pleasure.

The day he slipped completely to the other side, Mr. Windspir could finally hold his daughters. He could touch their hands and stroke his fingers through their hair. Also, he could feel the pull of the White. The sisters walked with their father through the field behind the farmhouse. When they reached the pasture fence, the sisters clutched a post, but Mr. Windspir kept his hands at his side. He stared into the White and felt the warmth of it pour into him.

"Won't you come?" he asked his daughters.

Violet and Henrietta followed their father's eyes. There were others in the White, their voices only barely out of range. When their father departed, he would be among them, and they would be left with the shadows of their living sisters.

"Won't you come?" Mr. Windspir repeated.

Violet and Henrietta stared into the White, tilted their

faces towards the warmth they didn't know was warmth. And then they shook their heads.

Won't you stay? they wanted to ask, but they knew the answer. He would not.

"I pity the others," Mr. Windspir said to his new-found daughters as he climbed the fence. "Their deaths such lonely times, such desolate times, only their bodies attended to. That they could have had what I had..." And then he leaned into the White, his feet slipping off the fence post. He floated there, suspended, until the White began to glimmer through his body, until the dark contours of his face turned to shine, until he was completely overtaken. Completely gone.

Violet dug a stone from the earth and carved a *D* in the post her father had stood on. Beside it she carved a *W*. And then together the spirit sisters turned away.

THE WINDSPIR SISTERS' HOME FOR THE DYING

The living Windspirs leaned over the shell of their father. Being nurses, the sisters had witnessed a number of passings in their short lives, but never had they seen one quite like this. If someone were to cast Mr. Windspir's death mask, the emotion captured would be jubilation.

"He's already gone," Violet announced when she and Henrietta returned to the house.

The living sisters nodded. They were thinking, and their thoughts were the same. It was Sarah who first voiced them. "Might there be a way to provide this type of comfort to others?"

The living sisters made the arrangements. They cleared from Mr. Windspir's bedroom all evidence of their father, each selecting only one memento. Elizabeth: a copy of *Swiss Family Robinson*, leather-bound in emerald green. A hubbed spine, end sheets of moiré fabric, a red silk ribbon page marker. A book Mr. Windspir had read aloud to his daughters numerous times during their childhood. Sarah: a half-empty cologne bottle. Maude: Mr. Windspir's lucky nickel, heads and tails both worn smooth. Isabelle: the nightdress in Mr. Windspir's sock drawer—their mother's—which she had discovered while scooping his socks—all black, all hand-darned—into a bag for charity. Violet and Henrietta had for years known about the presence of the nightgown, had for years seen their father primarily through the items in his possession. And yet their living sisters did not ask them if there was anything they wanted to keep for themselves. Henrietta tucked his childhood stamp album into the back of a kitchen drawer, but it did not escape her sisters' boxes and was eventually carted away. She did not protest.

The furniture and bed linens were kept, the family Bible, a pile of magazines, a stack of yellowed handkerchiefs the sisters employed as rags. They hung curtains from the ceiling, parcelling their father's room into four small cubicles. Mr. Windspir's bed and dresser were arranged in one, cots were purchased for the others. They put another bed in the pantry and another in the mud room. For the cost of materials, a carpenter—who credited the care of the Windspir sisters for his daughter's recovery from diphtheria—added an extension to the back porch to accommodate a further three beds. When they learned of the sisters' intentions, neighbours delivered linens and blankets, also teapots, novels, vases of dried flowers, lamps, rocking chairs, and embroidered Bible verses.

Violet and Henrietta watched the preparations with trepidation. They thought it inappropriate to discourage their living sisters from anything that would amount to more of their time spent at the Windspir homestead. And though they were unsure what this might entail, when Elizabeth—who had become the ringleader in the endeavour—asked Henrietta and Violet whether they were prepared to tend to the spirits of the dying as they had tended to their own father's spirit, Violet and Henrietta said they would.

Two months after Mr. Windspir's death, the first patient, a Margaret Remple, who suffered from dropsy as well as dementia, was welcomed into the home. She was a widow, and the mother of the chaplain. Those who had only recently made her acquaintance, the sisters included, considered her a kindly woman.

Violet and Henrietta could see Mrs. Remple as little more than a faint outline. The woman was accommodated in Mr. Windspir's bed, and rarely left it. They were not much affected by her presence, and though they were mildly annoyed by their sisters' preoccupation with this stranger, that in itself was no reason to protest. One by one the other cots were filled, and Henrietta and Violet's trepidation turned to tolerance. And then Mrs. Remple lost consciousness.

THE SHARING OF SPACE

Violet and Henrietta were in their sisters' bedroom, watching Isabelle, Maude, and Elizabeth sleep as Sarah performed the night rounds. This was a task the living sisters had hoped Violet and Henrietta would execute, but the spirit sisters were limited by their inability to hear and clearly see the patients.

Violet was remarking on this particular good fortune when Mrs. Remple wandered in. She had shucked her ailing body; this was apparent by the grace with which she moved and that she arrived through the wall rather than the door. Also that she was alarmingly visible.

"Are you the dead Windspir girls?" Mrs. Remple asked.

Violet and Henrietta associated bluntness with discourtesy. Had they the need to breathe, they would have inhaled sharply. Had they sensations in their bodies, they would have felt their skin prickle. "We are Violet and Henrietta," Violet said.

"Am I dead?"

The sisters did not know. Unconscious or dead, their father had looked no different. All that changed, in fact, was his fixation with the White. Violet supposed they could take Mrs. Remple outside and see if she flung herself from the fence, but Henrietta proposed a different course of action. "You could check your body."

Together the three of them passed through the wall into Mr. Windspir's room. The sisters hadn't been inside since Mrs. Remple's arrival, and they were taken aback by the transformation. They had expected something resembling the Remming Hospital — a place they remembered faintly from their own time there, but also knew from their sisters' stories. A place that was sparse and white and sterile. Instead, the colours in the room were riotous. Paintings hung from the walls, flowers bloomed in vases on every flat surface. Faint figures shifted and stretched in all four quilt-draped beds.

"It's horrible," Henrietta whispered as Violet barrelled through the outside wall. Then she turned to Mrs. Remple. "Your body is moving, so you must be alive."

"Christ," Mrs. Remple said, and Henrietta winced at this vain usage of the Lord's name, though she wasn't sure she believed in the Lord as her sisters did. If He existed, why had He not come to introduce Himself?

"I've endured that wretched body long enough," Mrs. Remple said. "I should smother myself with a pillow. Though I expect the details of my death will be shared with my son in the afterlife." Henrietta had seen the chaplain's faint outline daily, and had heard her sisters comment on how pious he was, and how handsome. Mrs. Remple turned to Henrietta. "If you were to assist..."

"Oh, no," Henrietta said. She was quite certain Elizabeth had meant something different when she asked Henrietta to tend to Mrs. Remple's spirit. Though obviously the woman was distressed. Obviously her spirit needed tending. She would need to wake Elizabeth and ask for direction.

And she was about to, when Mrs. Remple's spirit coiled into a sharp black kernel then shrieked through the air and into the old woman's faint, gaping mouth. In the next room, the living sisters began to stir, awoken by Mrs. Remple's screeches about ghosts.

Henrietta found Violet in front of the house, on the porch swing.

"We'll claim we neither saw nor heard her," Violet said.

"We did, though."

Violet grabbed Henrietta's hand with both of hers. "Henny, just think about what happens if we admit that."

The living sisters were pleased that Henrietta and Violet had proved capable of communicating with a patient's spirit self, but displeased with the direction these communications had taken.

"You are supposed to be a comfort," Elizabeth said. She had directed Sarah to settle Mrs. Remple with a

sedative dissolved in camomile tea and called a sisters'
meeting in the bedroom.

"How could we comfort her? I could barely see her,"
said Violet.

Though Henrietta also wished to be free from these
new intruders, the pledge she'd made to Elizabeth super-
seded her own desires. She could not go through with
Violet's plan. "I saw her," she admitted.

"Well, I guess all this comforting will be up to Henny,"
Violet said. And then she glided towards the wall and
slipped outside.

Henrietta imagined her sister storming the property
line. She imagined the words she was likely whittling into
needles, in preparation for their next encounter. And then
she turned to her living sisters. "How do I comfort them?"

"Isn't it odd that Violet couldn't see Maggie when you
could?" Maude said. Maude maintained that the use of the
patients' Christian names created a soothing familiarity.
The adoption of the nickname *Maggie* was calculated—
chosen to prove her methods had led to an authentic relationship. But the tone of her statement proved something
else: that the animosity that had developed between Maude
and Violet over the smashed porcelain doll—a treasure only
Maude had ever played with—had not completely faded.

"How do I comfort them?" Henrietta asked again.

"You helped Father," Isabelle said. "Just do whatever
it was you did for him."

Mr. Windspir had been content with the company of his lost children, but for the patients, this company was not enough. They wanted answers: How much longer did they have? What would happen next?

Of course, these were questions that Violet and Henrietta did not know the answers to. Not that Violet would have responded if she did. Her routine was always the same: when she came upon the spirit self of a patient, she would direct her gaze at something beyond him or her and pass right through.

Henrietta developed a routine also. She would gesture beyond the property line. She would admit that she had never been outside the Windspir homestead, aside from her six-day stint at the Remming Hospital, but that she had watched her father disappear into the White. She would be sure to mention that he had appeared content.

This was all she could do, but according to the dying it was not enough. They wanted evidence of lost loved ones, proof of an afterlife that extended beyond the haunting of one's own homestead, tales of her encounters with God. Violet suggested that Henrietta make up such stories. *It's not as though they'll come back to argue with you when they find out the truth. And if they do, at least you'll know.*

"Maybe *you* could do that," Henrietta suggested. She could not lie to the patients, but Violet had proved comfortable with dishonesty.

"How can I?" Violet asked. "I can't see them."

The spirits of the dying came and went at all hours. They arrived individually and in groups. They were ornery and demanding, or grief-stricken, or afraid. They were exhausting. Henrietta had no need for sleep, and yet she began to crave it. What she wanted more than anything was to turn the dying off. Her living sisters were not sympathetic. They reminded Henrietta that they *did* require sleep, and that they were not receiving much. That while the dying surely required a great deal when they were their spirit selves, in their bodies they required even more. There were fluids to administer, fluids to extract, fluids to swab. There were medications to dispense, fresh linens to dispense, reassurances to dispense. There were meals to prepare, meals to purée, meals to spoon-feed. There were wounds to dress, tears to staunch, attention to provide.

Violet was also not sympathetic. She had asserted the patients' invisibility from the beginning; she had given her sister an out. But Henrietta had chosen not to take it.

THE ARRIVAL OF BRIAN ANDERSON

Brian Anderson was a farmer, a farmer's son, and a farmer's grandson. He had learned to hand-roll a cigarette when he was nine. He was now forty years old and had never married.

He was a coarse man, mothered by a woman who had tired of child rearing well before he was born, raised instead by a litter of brothers. And though the Windspir sisters had also been brought up without a woman's influence, Mr. Windspir had been attentive to a number of things that rarely occupy single men — table manners, for instance. The importance of saying *Bless you* after a sneeze. How clothes should be pressed, and collars starched. That cleanliness is next to Godliness.

The living sisters were not taken with Brian Anderson. First, it was difficult to conduct a conversation while coughing and wheezing, and so he said little. Second, he still insisted on smoking, something that created a most distasteful chore. The chore of assisting Brian Anderson from his bed, absorbing his weight as he shuffled towards the door, accompanying him to the porch swing, constructing cigarettes under his direction, watching him suck hungrily, and ducking his exhales. This task was repeated at least three times an hour when Brian Anderson was awake, and each time he rang the small brass bell beside his bed, the sisters would lunge for brooms, for bedpans, for any alternate task that would excuse them.

Faced with Brian Anderson, the living Windspirs missed their father even more. And surely Brian Anderson could detect their resistance to him. His cot was in the windowless pantry, separated from the other patients and their discomfort, their discussions, their bouquet-wielding visitors, by a thick brocade curtain that remained closed.

When Brian Anderson slipped to the other side for the first time, he walked straight into Violet Windspir. "You're not a nurse," he said. The living sisters all wore their hair in tight buns, all wore white skirts and blouses and sensible shoes. All strode through the house with purpose, their posture so faultless one would have thought they had practised with books perched atop their heads. Violet lay on the grass with her arms tucked under her head. She was not wearing a nurse's uniform, though Brian wasn't sure what exactly she *was* wearing. His eyes had difficulty focusing, and though he could quite clearly see Violet Windspir, he could also see through her, to the dandelions that sprang up among the brittle shag of grass.

Violet didn't respond, and Brian Anderson sat beside her. He stretched out his pointer finger to test if she were a solid thing. When his hand passed through her arm, a jolt travelled the length of his body.

And then another sister arrived, another he could both see and see through. "She doesn't hear you," Henrietta said. "And no, she's not a nurse." Though the living Windspirs always spoke softly, always maintained eye contact, this Windspir's voice was sharp and her gaze flitted between him and her sister on the ground.

"Am I dead, then?" he asked. For of course Brian Anderson had heard of the Windspir sextet. And though he had been kept apart from the other patients, he had heard rumours that the lost Windspirs remained on the Windspir property to tend to the spirits of the dead.

But Henrietta had learned to tell the difference between a dying patient and a dead one. The dead had no time for questions, no time for worry or fear. She shook her head.

The sister on the ground lifted her hand and placed it down again, letting it fall through his. "This one I do hear," Violet said, her gaze fixed to the dying man's face.

THE LONG DEATH OF BRIAN ANDERSON

After his initial meeting with Violet, Brian Anderson lost consciousness regularly. Henrietta suspected that this was not coincidental. More than once she caught Violet in the medicine cabinet. She recovered pill bottles from under Brian's pillow when he and her sister were lounging by the fence line. She overheard a conversation between the two about the effects of holding one's breath.

She brought Violet and Brian's relationship to the attention of her living sisters. She was concerned, she said. Violet was certainly providing Brian Anderson with comfort, but it was a reckless comfort. Because while she was glad her sister was happy (and Violet maintained this to be true), Brian Anderson was no more than a visitor to the Windspir homestead. He would die, and he would leave, and Violet would be heartbroken.

Maude said the relationship between Violet and Brian Anderson was proof that Violet could see the dying, could hear the dying, and that she had been lying when she claimed otherwise. And furthermore, it was not Violet's job to administer medication.

Isabelle said it was not possible that Violet and Brian Anderson were in a relationship. It was not possible that anyone would willingly enter into a relationship with Brian Anderson.

Elizabeth said it did not matter how Violet chose to provide comfort. At least she was providing it. The burden of Brian Anderson had been lifted somewhat. Henrietta could stand to learn something from her spirit sister.

Sarah thought Henrietta's concerns were legitimate. She did not want Violet to get hurt. But when Brian Anderson was in his spirit state, Sarah was not required to interact with him. So she said nothing.

Henrietta tried to broach the issue with Violet herself, but her sister was not receptive. "The heart wants what the heart wants," Violet said. But Violet was not the only spirit sister to have worked her way through the Windspir bookshelf; Henrietta was equally familiar with this line of poetry, and unconvinced of its truth.

"We don't have hearts," Henrietta said. "Technically." But then Brian Anderson appeared between them, and he and Violet drifted to the far edge of the property, where they lay side by side in the grass with their hands overlapped.

THE (ACCOMPANIED) DEPARTURE OF BRIAN ANDERSON

A fortnight after Brian Anderson first lost consciousness, he died. And like all those who had passed before him, he felt the pull of the White.

Violet stood with him at the edge of the property.

They held hands — which was only now possible. She watched Brian tilt his face towards the White the same way Mr. Windspir had. "You can't go," she said. She had never missed anyone who had left, not even her father. And though she had no body, she still felt a knot of tightness, a shiver of cold, a heavy throbbing. Except these feelings were not limited the way they are in a living person: trapped in the throat or pressed up against the diaphragm. They were encompassing. She glanced behind her at Henrietta, who stood at the edge of the copse of trees with her jaw set hard and her arms crossed over her chest.

"Not alone," Brian said. He took a step towards the fence, tugging Violet with him. The White glowed brighter than Violet remembered. It reflected off Brian's bare arms so they shone. The hair on his forearms was the colour of the dry grass on the edge of the homestead, but soft as sunlight.

"My sisters..." Violet said. She could feel Henrietta's gaze even though her eyes were fixed on Brian.

"Your sisters should want you to be happy," Brian said.

"But Henrietta..."

"Wasn't getting any help from you to begin with."

Violet let Brian pull her against him. Her hips skimmed the fence as she tucked into his arms. She squeezed Brian's hand, then dropped it and pushed herself back. "Just wait," she said.

Henrietta was already beside her. "You can't go with him."

"We could both go," Violet said.

"We made a promise to our sisters."

"Our sisters should want us to be happy," Violet echoed.

"I am happy," Henrietta said, though whether or not this was true was unclear, even to Henrietta herself. "And we should want them to be happy too."

"Tell them I do. Tell them I love them. Tell them I'll see you all soon." Brian had climbed to the top of a fence post. Violet took his hand and he hoisted her up beside him.

"No," Henrietta screamed. She lunged for Violet's leg, but when she felt the magnetism of the White, she ripped herself backwards and away. She watched as Brian and Violet tipped over the fence, hung suspended in the air, Violet's body curled into Brian so that she couldn't see her sister's face. Couldn't see as the White glimmered from her cheeks, then leaked from her eye sockets, couldn't see her expression the moment before she was overtaken.

THE LONELINESS OF HENRIETTA WINDSPIR

After Henrietta's wailing alerted the sisters to Violet's departure, Elizabeth called a sisters' meeting, but their remaining spirit sister was too saturated with grief to participate. Though she sat on the bedroom floor beside her sisters, Henrietta did not utter a word, and appeared to them to be wobbling—invisible to visible and back again. Sarah sat beside her. She was unable to give her sister a hug, though she longed to do so. She hoped that her proximity, at least, was comforting. It was all she had to offer. Had she acted sooner, she could have offered more: support for Henrietta's concerns, an intervention. She could have confided to Violet that there had been men she had cared for also, men who had provided attention she had been tempted to return. But, she would have explained, she had always weighed the love these suitors promised against the sacrifices required if she were to claim it. And in every case she had made the right choice: namely, her sisters.

But now it was too late. Violet had made a forever leap with a man she barely knew. With the first man who had expressed an interest. With such a man as Brian Anderson.

Isabelle was sympathetic, but perplexed. How could Henrietta be certain that Violet wouldn't return from the White? Never having ventured beyond the fenceline herself, her knowledge was limited. And was Henrietta implying that there were levels of death — that Violet was somehow more dead than Henrietta was? Did the other sisters support this hypothesis?

"She's gone for good," Elizabeth said. And because Elizabeth was an expert on most matters, or at least professed to be, this truth was accepted.

"It's not like this is a tragedy," Maude said. "Violet was already dead. And we'll likely see her when we die ourselves." It was Maude who had carved their initials into a fence post: *VW, BA*. The ninth and tenth pair of initials, Brian being the eighth patient to die and Violet being the second Windspir to disappear into the White. "In all probability she's with Mother and Father. And with Brian Anderson." Maude made no effort to stifle her snort of derision.

Henrietta wobbled invisible again. For a long stretch of silence Elizabeth and Isabelle watched the space where she had sat, Sarah glared at Maude, Maude pressed her cuticles down with her thumbnail. When it became clear Henrietta would not be returning to the meeting, Maude spoke again. "She wasn't even contributing."

"She wasn't," Elizabeth agreed. "But now Henrietta is in no shape to do so either. Instead of providing comfort, her howls and moans will inspire fear. We need to be sympathetic, and accommodating. We need to give her a reprieve from the demands of the dying. Think about the problem on our hands if she decides to follow."

"We need to be sympathetic because she's our sister," Sarah said. "Because we love her. Not because it will be inconvenient if she decides to jump the fence herself."

"Of course," Elizabeth said. "But we must also be practical."

Isabelle and Maude nodded. Sarah closed her eyes. "So we stop taking on patients," Isabelle said.

"Rather, we have a patient remedy the situation," said Elizabeth. "And I know the one."

The next steps Elizabeth took unilaterally. She went to the bedside of one Mrs. Higginbotham, and requested she step into Henrietta's role for a week or two once she herself slipped completely into the spirit world. Mrs. Higginbotham was the perfect candidate because she was in the gravest condition—not expected to last beyond the week. She was a meek and mild woman who had spent her life appeasing a domineering husband and a domineering son. Henrietta had met Mrs. Higginbotham a number of times previously and their interactions had been pleasant, and also pleasantly brief. In her forays into the spirit world, Mrs. Higginbotham sat at the fenceline and stared into the White. She did not ask questions. And she did not ask questions of Elizabeth now. She did not even pause to consider the request. She agreed.

THE ASSISTANCE OF MRS. HIGGINBOTHAM

Occasionally, when an individual is granted power for the first time, they become intoxicated by it. This is the case for the dead as well as the living. As a dying woman—and even previously as a healthy woman—Mrs. Higginbotham was timid and docile. As a spirit, she was a tyrant.

Initially, Henrietta appreciated this. Mrs. Higginbotham didn't allow the patients near the last remaining spirit sister, and Henrietta no longer had to worry about being accosted as she sat sullenly in the woods. Mrs. Higginbotham insisted on remaining with the patients for the duration of their ventures in the spirit world. She ordered they recount all their insecurities and fears so she could comfort them. But as Mrs. Higginbotham settled into her role, she demanded more of Henrietta than any of the dying ever had. Mrs. Higginbotham kept Henrietta apprised of the details of her often lengthy interactions with the patients. As Henrietta was the only spirit the living sisters were able to communicate with, Henrietta was expected to pass these updates on, a task she rarely performed. Worst of all, though, Mrs. Higginbotham believed that it was vital that together she and Henrietta develop appropriate, factual responses to the patients' litany of questions. As the most frequent question was about the White, Henrietta was therefore obliged to share all she knew.

Henrietta offered Violet's solution: Mrs. Higginbotham could lie. *It's not as though they'll come back to argue with you when they find out the truth.* She didn't want to go near the White, or speculate about the White, or rehash what had happened when Violet entered it. But Mrs. Higginbotham claimed all this was essential.

It was not only Henrietta who took issue with Mrs. Higginbotham; the patients weren't particularly fond of her either. Why, they wondered, could they not enjoy some solitude in the spirit world? Some space and quiet to reflect on their lives? Some time to process? Some time without Mrs. Higginbotham's incessant chatter boring into their souls?

Elizabeth called a sisters' meeting. While Sarah tucked herself tightly against Henrietta's faint outline and directed calm, soothing thoughts, Elizabeth gave instructions on how Henrietta was to approach Mrs. Higginbotham with the patients' complaints.

"I want nothing to do with this," Henrietta said as she passed directly through Elizabeth and then the outside wall.

"It's been over a week," Maude said. "How long can we allow Henrietta to act like this?"

"Imagine what it must be like for her," Sarah said. "Stuck here her entire life, Violet her only real company. Then the house fills with strangers she's expected to comfort, Violet abandons her for Brian Anderson, Mrs. Higginbotham accosts her. The only escape available to her is the White, and she's too loyal to take it."

"The thing is, Sarah, I can't imagine," Maude said. "None of us can claim to imagine what her life is like. But I expect it's quite pleasant: coming and going as she pleases, no real responsibilities."

"Meanwhile, the problem remains," Isabelle said. "How are we supposed to deal with Mrs. Higginbotham?"

"There's only one way." And from her pocket Elizabeth pulled the same bottle of pills that Violet had once thieved for Brian Anderson.

MAUDE'S VISIT TO THE SPIRIT WORLD

Elizabeth was willing to enter the spirit world but as the self-appointed director of the Home for the Dying, she proposed another sister should go in her stead. Sarah and Isabelle were fearful and therefore reluctant. Maude, however, was mostly intrigued.

She was not disappointed by the experience. Abandoning one's body provided a sort of freedom Maude had never before experienced. She would have been content to float aimlessly around the property, passing through solid objects, enjoying the sensation of moving without any physical effort, but as she was unsure of the length of time available to her, she got directly to the business at hand. She set out to find Mrs. Higginbotham.

Maude stumbled across Henrietta first, lying on her back in the woods. She both saw her and saw through her at once, as was usual, though Henrietta was much more sharply defined than she'd ever appeared in the past.

Henrietta sat up immediately. "Are you ill, Maude?"

"Just visiting," Maude said.

Of course, Brian Anderson had proved that one could enter the spirit world unnaturally. And though Henrietta had lately wished her sisters would follow his example, would provide her the comfort of their proximity, it was clear this particular visit was not for Henrietta's sake.

She lay back down. "Visitors aren't welcome."

"You're not who I've come to see." Maude pushed through the oak behind her sister and almost barrelled into Mrs. Higginbotham, who was streaking towards her.

"I was under the impression that communication with you living ones was impossible. Unless, of course, you're dying? Which one are you, anyways?"

"I'm Maude. And no. I've only come to talk." The Mrs. Higginbotham who had been a patient was strikingly different from the Mrs. Higginbotham in front of her. Age hadn't wrecked havoc on this woman's features, nor had arthritis masked her grace, but it was more than a physical thing. This woman had confidence. She spoke before being spoken to. She looked Maude in the eyes directly and did not shrink back when her gaze was returned.

"I would have requested a conversation sooner, had I been informed you could slip into the spirit world at a whim. I have a number of concerns..." Mrs. Higginbotham began.

Upon Mrs. Higginbotham's arrival, Henrietta sat up to watch, but when Maude glanced in her direction, she lay back down and closed her eyes.

"Since my time is limited, I'd prefer to go first," Maude said. "The thing is, while no doubt the patients appreciate your efforts to comfort them, many of them would like some time by themselves when they arrive in the spirit world. To process."

Mrs. Higginbotham snorted. "That's what you'd like me to provide them with — time to process? And what about the fact that I'm unequipped to answer their most pressing questions? That your sister refuses even to discuss the White?"

"The White," Maude repeated. Of course, she had quite forgotten about it, but now that she remembered, she wanted to proceed to the fenceline immediately. "Show me."

THE ILL-FATED PLAN

"I've tried to convince others to dip their toes in, so to speak, and then report back," said Mrs. Higginbotham, "yet I am singular among the dead in self-control. They plunge in immediately, more often than not. In fact, though I request they carve their own initials, I often must do so myself post-departure."

"And you don't feel a pull?" asked Maude, who didn't feel anything in particular herself. Though the White was fascinating. And not entirely white, either, white being void of colour, while whatever it was surrounding the homestead was darker, more tumultuous in places, and in other places static and flat.

"I feel it," said Mrs. Higginbotham. "Which is why I haven't attempted such a toe dip myself."

"Perhaps I should," Maude said, because at that moment she couldn't think of a single reason why this mightn't be a good idea, and countless reasons why it was necessary. For instance, was it not possible that rather than being an endless substance, the White was more a curtain? That Maude could push through and view all that was underneath?

Mrs. Higginbotham beamed at Maude. She clapped her hands. "Oh, of course, you must."

Maude pulled herself on top of a fence post. Pressed against the White, she felt its magnetism, but only barely. She tried to lean, but the White provided no resistance and she was afraid she might fall—either in or off. She straightened up and tried to content herself with peering. Except that there was nothing to peer at—only more of the same.

"I'm going to go deeper," Maude said to Mrs. Higginbotham, who was hovering a short distance from the fenceline. "If I appear to be slipping away, you will clasp my ankle and reel me in."

"Yes, of course," said Mrs. Higginbotham, who had been in the spirit world long enough that she should have been aware that the dead can only touch, let alone clasp, one another.

Mrs. Higginbotham stood at the edge of the fence. Maude peered, then peered further, then she leaned. Her feet slipped from the post and she hung there, suspended. Mrs. Higginbotham jumped for her leg, but could not make contact.

"Astounding," Maude sighed.

At this moment Henrietta stepped from the edge of the forest. "Maude! Get back!"

"Yes, yes, I can hear you," Maude said, though these words seemed not to be directed at Henrietta. The White had begun to glimmer through her arms and legs.

Mrs. Higginbotham clambered up a fence post and stretched for Maude's glowing ankle as it floated higher. She leapt for it. And then she was suspended also.

Henrietta reached the fenceline. "Maude," she screamed. Her sister was pulsing with white. Maude sighed—or moaned? Her expression was hidden by the glow of her face. And then, in one bright flash, she and Mrs. Higginbotham both disappeared.

THE FALLOUT

No more than a minute passed before Sarah ran from the house, shouting Maude's name.

"She's not breathing," she screamed when she saw Henrietta hovering in front of her. "Why is she not breathing?"

"Because she's gone," Henrietta said. "Into the White with Mrs. Higginbotham."

"How is that possible?" Sarah demanded. "She's not dead."

"Wasn't. Is now," said Henrietta. When Violet had disappeared, she had felt the wound as something raw and weeping. Now she felt only numb. She picked up a rock and moved to the fence post that Maude had stood on only moments before. *MW*, she carved. She returned to Sarah, who sat rocking back and forth on the grass. "Emily? Was that Mrs. Higginbotham's Christian name?"

The back door slammed and Elizabeth and Isabelle charged down the steps.

"Where is Maude?" Elizabeth demanded. Then her eyes settled on Sarah. "No. No, it's impossible."

The three living Windspirs sat clutching hands as Henrietta recounted the details. "It's given me an idea, anyways," she concluded. "I will have all the patients leap into the White when I first encounter them, as a way to stop their hearts and reduce the frequency and duration of visits."

"Henrietta," Elizabeth said. But before she could

lecture her sister on the capriciousness of such an action, Henrietta faded from view.

Elizabeth and Isabelle stood, but Sarah — displaying an uncharacteristic inattention to propriety — remained curled in a tight fist on the ground. Her uniform was crumpled and smudged with dirt. She would not speak when spoken to.

Elizabeth and Isabelle wandered through the woods, then traced the fenceline, though they were both aware that such a search was pointless. Their spirit sister was adept at remaining invisible when it suited her. It was in fact possible that she had already leapt into the White, though her initials had not been scratched into any fence posts. This Elizabeth checked.

It seemed an appropriate occasion for a meeting, to discuss events, to decompress, but only Isabelle and Elizabeth would have willingly attended. Also, there was no time. The hospice beds were full. In the front room, all the patient bells chimed in unison. The tasks that had filled the days of four living sisters would now have to be undertaken by three — by two until Sarah recovered.

THE SISTERS' SUFFERING

For Sarah, the loss of Maude was overwhelming. It twisted together with the loss of Violet, forming a thick rope that coiled around her chest and made it difficult to breathe. But it was not only her lost sisters she mourned.

There was also Henrietta, alone now. Henrietta, who had slipped invisible before Sarah could offer any comfort. Not that Sarah had much to offer her spirit sister. She could not hold her hand, or take her into her arms—at least not while she was alive. Sarah's ears were shut to the sounds of the patients' bells, ringing to call for medication, for water glasses, for comfort. In her mind, her worst fear spooled out: Henrietta atop a fence post leaping into a void.

But Henrietta was not atop a post, only near one. Not leaping into the White, but rather trying to scrape it away with her gaze, attempting to see beyond. She could see nothing. Were Violet and Maude together? Was her father with them also? And the mother she had barely met? There wasn't anything she could have done to make Violet stay, but she felt entirely responsible for Maude's departure. Had Henrietta agreed to approach Mrs. Higginbotham with the patients' complaints, Maude would not have had reason to cross into the spirit world. But more importantly: if Henrietta had mourned more quietly the loss of Violet, Elizabeth would not have requested Mrs. Higginbotham's services to begin with. Mrs. Higginbotham would have leapt into the White immediately after death, and Henrietta would have remembered her only as a sad and silent woman, if she remembered her at all.

She was envisioning this alternate history when a patient passed through the wall of the farmhouse and drifted towards the fenceline: a tall woman with long white hair in a braid that hung past her waist. Henrietta had not seen her before, and now had to consider her options: to encourage the intruder to throw herself into the White, or to ignore her—just as Violet would have done. Or, more appropriately, to do what her sisters had requested from the beginning: comfort this dying woman to the best of her abilities. But just as Henrietta resolved to do precisely that, the woman climbed a fence post and stepped off. As she floated, the glow overtaking her body, Henrietta had a chance to examine her face. It was rapturous.

Meanwhile, in the farmhouse, Elizabeth and Isabelle moved from patient to patient. Neither could remember the last time she had slept longer than an hour, that she had sat for a meal, that she had observed silence. In the beds were nine patients, some of them strides from death and others pressed tightly against it. At that moment, most of them were rooted in the living world, as evidenced by the needs they were expressing. Needs too great for Elizabeth and Isabelle to attend to alone.

Only one patient bell was silent: the one of Mrs. Morris in the mud room, who had arrived only the day before. Mrs. Morris had been up most of the night, delirious with pain. Elizabeth had promised another dose of morphine in the morning. Promised, and forgot. She pulled back the curtain to check on the woman and found her finally peaceful. Found her, in fact, dead.

"Isabelle," Elizabeth shouted, and Isabelle appeared with a bedpan in each hand. She set the pans on the floor and took a step towards the woman, hovered her cheek above Mrs. Morris's mouth, touched her fingers to her neck to locate her pulse. Then she righted herself and nodded at her sister.

"Henrietta pushed her into the White," Elizabeth said.

Before Isabelle could argue, could say the dead could not even touch the living, Elizabeth clarified. "Figuratively. Exactly as she said she would."

Isabelle too remembered her spirit sister's threat, yet she did not believe Henrietta capable of such recklessness. "Mrs. Morris was very ill. I'm sure she died entirely on her own."

"No," Elizabeth said. "We need to do something."

Isabelle, who understood precisely what Elizabeth intended, shook her head. "I'm not taking those pills," she said. "And we're too busy in this world to go into the next." Her gaze drifted again to Mrs. Morris. "If Henrietta sped up her death, it was a kindness. The poor woman had suffered enough."

"It's not up to us to determine the timeline." Elizabeth marched towards the bedroom, Isabelle trailing behind her.

Isabelle could not allow Elizabeth to take Maude's path: to turn a visit to the spirit world into a final exit from the living one. For once she resolved to overrule her sister; Elizabeth would stay because Isabelle would demand it. And if that was not enough, which it likely wasn't, Isabelle would pocket the pills and dispose of them: out the window or down the drain. But as soon as Isabelle entered the bedroom, she saw Maude.

Isabelle watched as Elizabeth pushed Maude's body to the edge of her bed then lay beside her. Isabelle watched as Elizabeth squeezed Maude's hand and kissed her forehead. She watched with her mouth frozen shut and her feet planted in place. And then, when Elizabeth took the pills from the bedside table, placed four in her mouth, and washed them down with water from the glass their newly dead sister had sipped from only minutes earlier, Isabelle fled. The patient bells rang a racket.

Sarah was still outside, curled on the grass. She did not see the spirit self of her living sister walk past her. Her mind kept replaying the same images: Henrietta at the fenceline. Henrietta, jumping. And then she came to a decision. She stood and strode towards the shed beside the garden. She pulled out the hoes and shovels, abandoned since Mr. Windspir's death, forming a clear path to the hoses and ropes looped on hooks along the back wall.

THE SPIRIT WORLD ACCOMMODATES MORE

Elizabeth's exhaustion had been abandoned along with her body, and for the first time in months she felt restored. Her desire to experience this sensation overshadowed the need for an immediate search for her spirit sister. She closed her eyes and allowed herself a moment to revel in the absence of everything.

Meanwhile, Isabelle slipped ice cubes between chapped lips, she pressed cool cloths against burning brows, she stacked woollen sheets atop quaking bodies. Isabelle stroked hair, wiped drool, and whispered reassurances. And while thus engaged, she heard footsteps through the doorway, which could only be Sarah, risen from the grass at last. "Sarah," she called. But there was no response, only the sound of something being dragged the length of the hall. The bedroom door opened, then clicked shut.

Sarah pulled her bundle to the corner of the bedroom, then stood back. She had resolve, but what she needed was an immediate onslaught of courage. She turned to the bed. There was Maude, eyes closed, one arm drooped down, knuckles skimming the floor. Peaceful.

And beside her, Elizabeth.

As Sarah's mind conjured up a new terror, Elizabeth's chest rose, then fell. Sarah let out her breath and felt her body loosen. Elizabeth was asleep. She would awaken as capable as always. Everything in the living world would be fine.

In the front room, Isabelle mashed pills into food pur-ées, spooned purées into gaping mouths, and massaged throats into swallowing. Isabelle mopped spills, stripped sheets, emptied bedpans. And all the while she thought of Sarah—already devastated by the losses of Violet, of Maude—who had by now seen Elizabeth, lying motion-less. Would it be too much? Isabelle held up her hand to the barrage of patient complaints. "I need to check on my sister," she said.

When Sarah heard Isabelle's footsteps in the hall, she threw a quilt over her bundle. She waited for Isabelle to enter the bedroom, then pulled her sister towards her and concentrated on savouring their embrace.

Isabelle pulled away. She had dark circles under her eyes. Strands of hair had escaped her bun. Her dress was creased and there were specks of blood on the left sleeve. "Elizabeth is with Henrietta," she said. "Hopefully she'll be back soon."

"I thought she was asleep," Sarah said.

Isabelle's gaze turned in the direction of the chiming bells. "There's no time for sleep."

Sarah reached for Isabelle's hand and squeezed.

"Are you fine now?" Isabelle asked. "Will you help?"

"I'm going to help," Sarah said. She smiled at her sister, but she didn't move.

Isabelle shook her head. She left the room and Sarah closed the door behind her. There was much to do before Elizabeth returned.

Henrietta had seen Elizabeth as soon as she passed through the wall of the farmhouse. Before, when Maude arrived, she had initially assumed her living sister was ill, but she knew that Elizabeth had only come to meddle. She had not forgotten Elizabeth's lack of sympathy when Henrietta first brought up the problem of Violet and Brian Anderson. She had not forgotten that Mrs. Higginbotham was Elizabeth's idea. Nor had she forgiven her sister for these things. Let Elizabeth wander around the spirit world. Let her leer into the White. Henrietta did not intend to serve as either tour guide or whipping boy. She hid herself in the copse of trees and sneaked glances at her sister, hovering with her arms outstretched.

Finally, Elizabeth opened her eyes. She did not know how much time she had, and she could not squander another moment of it with her own enjoyment. She predicted Henrietta would be at the fenceline, either mourning Violet and Maude or lying in wait for other patients to encourage towards death.

Elizabeth headed for the edge of the property, and as she approached the fence, she had her first view of the White. She had imagined it would be brighter—a glaring she'd need to avert her eyes from—this because Mr. Windspir had mentioned the warmth. Elizabeth didn't feel warmth, or any sort of magnetism either. To her, the White was like low-lying clouds: billowing, shifting, ominous. She could not conceive why anyone would enter it willingly. She walked the length of the fenceline, but Henrietta wasn't there. Elizabeth wasn't sure whether to wait for her sister or search for her. As she pondered this, she sensed movement behind her. She turned and there was Henrietta, at the edge of the woods, her arms around another sister. Elizabeth's first thought was that Maude had returned from the White. But of course, it wasn't Maude.

THE HOME FOR THE DYING CLOSES

It wasn't long before all the people in Remming knew the story of the Windspir sisters, or at least a version. How a Mrs. Tate, or Taylor, or Tanner had arrived at the Home for the Dying with a bouquet of violets or an Edith Wharton paperback or a flask of brandy for her husband, or son, or father. How, after knocking repeatedly, she had let herself in. Her ensuing screams and quick retreat. How the neighbourhood men had pushed aside their dinner plates and armed themselves with carving knives or fire pokers or garden tools and set upon the house to investigate. And what they had found in the Windspir sisters' bedroom: one Windspir sawing at a rope with a steak knife, a rope that was looped around a ceiling beam and also the neck of her dead, but still warm, sister. A spilled bottle of pills on a bed that contained another two Windspirs: one whose pulse was slow and weak, the other whose pulse was non-existent and whose body was stiff and cold. How the police were called, and the coroner, and how soon the last two living sisters — the quartet turned duet — were carted off to where they belonged.

The people of Remming soon forgot about the comfort the Windspir sisters had provided their dying family members. They also forgot what the sisters had done, before that, for the living. It was fortunate, they said, that Mr. Windspir had not lived to see what had become of his daughters. Though most agreed that he bore some responsibility. No man could expect to raise up girls into women on his own.

There had once been six, the people reminded each other. The death of two a blessing, in retrospect. Maybe the doctors should not have strived so hard to save the others. Maybe there was a reason they were born weak— their bodies a match for their moral fibre. Some of the elderly tried to recall the phase of the moon on the evening of the birth, and convinced themselves it had been full; that the sisters' turn to lunacy should have been predicted. Of course, there were whispers about the devil.

As to how this story ended, the people of Remming could only guess; even if they had wanted to call on the Windspirs—out of compassion or curiosity—they could not have done so. Asylums were not a place for visitors; their conditions were intolerable for the well. But one could assume, and many did. As the days of purging and bloodletting were past, the sisters were likely turned comatose by opiates, by insulin shock therapy, by ice picks hammered through the top of their eye sockets— a psychic mercy killing. And in the spirit of that mercy, one could only hope their bodies had perished along with their minds.

Certainly they were no longer a danger. Even if they were one day released, they would be altered. And they would be sterilized. As perhaps their mother should have been. Though no one had more than a faded memory of Mrs. Windspir, and though it was wrong to speak ill of the dead, it was only natural to speculate.

A banker from the next county bought the Windspir homestead despite the rumours. The price was right. The house, unattractive and structurally unsound, was razed. The fence at the edge of the property—rotted, half collapsed, and gouged with hieroglyphics—was torn up and replaced with pickets. Painted white. The day after the new fence was completed, a pair of initials appeared scratched in the centre of it: *SW, HW.* Neighbourhood children, the new owner assumed, exerting some sort of claim. He had the letters sanded out and another coat of paint applied, erasing the trace of them altogether.

⚞ ACKNOWLEDGMENTS

Thank you to everyone at House of Anansi, particularly Janice Zawerbny for her insight, encouragement, support—and for taking a chance. Thank you to John Sweet for eradicating many of my errors before they made their way into the world.

Thank you to the literary journals that provided homes for earlier versions of these stories. In particular, thank you to Rilla Friesen at *Grain* for helping chase out the unessential from "Second Comings and Goings," and John Barton at *The Malahat Review* for his grammatical brilliance.

Winchester .30-.30 would not have been possible without "Bloody Falls of the Coppermine," by McKay Jenkins. *Electrocuting the Elephant* would not have been possible without "Topsy," by Michael Daly, nor without the sparks the amazing articles on Paul Karn's *Impolitic Eye* blog started in my mind. Thank you to the many Ronald Reagan biographers. Piles of your tomes covered my bed-side table during the first draft of "Double Dutch."

Resounding gratitude to my tenacious crew of fellow writers for their wisdom and expertise: Jason Brown, Jennifer Caloyeras, Lisa Baldissera, Paul Carlucci, Sarah Selecky, Una McDonnell, Zoe Stikeman, and most especially Buffy Cram for her exacting eye and valuable friendship, Carey Rudisill for her support and encouragement across the miles, and my first reader, Matthew J. Trafford, whose writer brain offers mine the best sort of kinship.

Zsuzsi Gartner has been a midwife and fairy godmother to many of these stories, not to mention a great friend to me. No thanks I give her will ever be enough.

Thank you to my family, especially Marnie McKay, for her support from the beginning, and for giving me time to write. Thank you to Angus, for inspiration and purpose. And thanks to Mike for more than I can list.

Louise Carson's SF fiction has been published in both
Irish and Irish-Canadian and Canadian, in
the anthology Daevas, Seasons, Antonia, Tales from
Tomorrow. Her nonfiction has garnered two nominations
for national ... the national magazine awards. She is
the author of the children's novel The Swanhild Story,
Paris Oaks ... She lives in Montreal with
her husband and son.

LAURA TRUNKEY's fiction has been published in journals and magazines across Canada, and was included in the anthology *Darwin's Bastards: Astounding Tales from Tomorrow*. Her non-fiction has garnered two honourable mentions at the National Magazine Awards. She is the author of the children's novel *The Incredibly Ordinary Danny Chandelier* (2008). She lives in Victoria, B.C., with her husband and son.